HIDE AND SEEK

UPSIDE ★ DOWN MAGIC

HIDE AND SEEK

by

Sarah
MLYNOWSKI,

Lauren
MYRACLE,

and

Emily
JENKINS

SCHOLASTIC PRESS/New York

ISBN 978-1-338-22155-8

10 9 8 7 6 5 4 3 2 1   20 21 22 23 24

Printed in the U.S.A. 23
First edition, July 2020

Book design by Abby Dening

Dedicated to the amazing young actors of the
Upside-Down Magic movie:
Izabela Rose, Siena Agudong, Alison Fernandez,
Elie Samouhi, Max Torina, and Yasmeen Fletcher

Nory was preparing to take a Big Test.

The Big Test, for the second time.

The first time had been a disaster.

Nory was in fifth grade. She liked sugary breakfast cereal. She wore bright clothes. She had big hair, brown skin, and a terrible singing voice. She was outspoken, but it was easy to hurt her feelings. Her magic talent was fluxing and her full name was Elinor Boxwood Horace.

Back in the summer before fifth grade, Nory's magic powers had bubbled up. All kids got their powers around age ten. Then they went to magic school.

In magic school, just like in ordinary school, you had to read and write and do science projects—but you also studied magic. The type of magic you studied depended on your talent. Everyone was labeled as one of the five Fs:

Flyers could fly or make things fly.

Flares had fire or heating magic.

Flickers could turn invisible or make other things invisible.

Fuzzies had animal magic and could communicate with animals. They might command a flock of geese or befriend a rhinoceros.

And Fluxers could turn themselves into animals. But not *all* animals. Not right away. Beginner Fluxers started by turning themselves into kittens. Then they learned to shift into puppies, hamsters, and other small domestic mammals before studying how to flux into large ones. Then they learned wild ones. And tricky ones. Non-mammals like fish, insects, and birds were especially hard.

Nory could actually do some large creatures already. Also, she had fluxed into two different fish, one insect, and a bluebird. Problem was, she didn't keep them in the right shape. Nory had upside-down magic.

That could have been no big deal in another family, but Nory's father was the headmaster of a very fancy private magic school called Sage Academy. It only admitted the students with the strongest magic. The strongest, most conventional magic.

Nory's sister, Dalia, went to Sage.

Nory's brother, Hawthorn, went to Sage.

And Nory had always been expected to go to Sage as well.

But on the day of the Big Test, she couldn't flux "properly." She jumbled up her animals. She added snake to her kitten to become a snitten. Then she added dragon to her kitten to become a dritten.

Even worse, Nory tended to lose track of her human mind when she fluxed. During the first Big Test, she had breathed fire at people. And she had almost eaten a unicorn.

Nory had been denied admission to Sage Academy. It had been the worst day ever.

After that, Father had sent Nory to live in the town of Dunwiddle with Aunt Margo, Nory's mother's sister. (Nory's mother had died when Nory was very young.) The public school near Aunt Margo had a trial program just starting up, for kids with upside-down magic. Nory went there for fifth grade, instead of going to Sage.

It had turned out great. There'd been a few bumps here and there, sure, but Aunt Margo was fun to live with. She was nowhere near as strict as Father. She ordered pizza in for dinner almost every night and let Nory eat sugary breakfast cereal out of the box. She was a flyer who ran her own flying taxi service.

Right away, Nory had made a best friend. His

name was Elliott Cohen, and he was an Upside-Down Flare. Elliott could flare just a tiny bit and also had ice powers.

A bit later, Nory had made *another* best friend, Pepper Phan. Pepper was an Upside-Down Fuzzy, which meant that animals didn't love her the way they loved typical Fuzzies. Instead, they ran away from Pepper in terror.

Nory adored her teacher, Ms. Starr, and liked the other kids in her class. There were eight students total in Upside-Down Magic, and as a rule, they stood up for one another. Sometimes the typical kids were mean, especially a Flare named Lacey Clench. But overall, Nory was happy at Dunwiddle.

And then Father had come along, tra la la, and said, "Oh, hey, here's a fun idea! Remember that test you failed, Nory? Why don't you take it again?!"

But not in those words.

Last night, Father had driven two hours to the town of Dunwiddle. Over cups of tea, he had explained to Nory and Aunt Margo that one of the Sage fifth graders was moving to Australia. There would be an opening in the fifth grade, starting in January.

Father wanted Nory to apply.

Well, *re*apply.

Now that Nory's magic was under better control, and since she'd had a great report card, he thought she could get in.

Father usually got what he wanted. He expected his children to be obedient, and he believed he knew what was best for them. Nory wasn't sure she wanted to go to Sage Academy, but he was so bossy. She let him drive her home without protesting.

She slept in her old bed, which felt cozy but also too small. She got up in the morning and put on a dress.

She squashed her hair into two neat braids.

She ate blueberries, whole wheat toast, and a soft-boiled egg for breakfast.

It was like nothing had changed—even though *everything* had changed. She wasn't the same Nory as she had been before Ms. Starr's Upside-Down Magic class. But here she was, back in her same old life.

She washed her dishes. She brushed her teeth.

And she went to take the test.

Now, on Thursday night when she should have been watching TV, Nory stood on the stage of Sage Academy's Hall of Magic and Performance, trembling. The ceilings were decorated with dragons and unicorns. The seats were dark purple velvet. The curtains on the side of the stage were gold.

A group of teachers in suits looked back at her. They asked her to try all five of the Fs, since some rare kids were double talents. First flaring, then fuzzying, then flickering, then flying.

Nory couldn't do any of those, because she didn't have that kind of magic, so she just politely shook her head.

Then they asked to see her fluxing magic.

She did *not* show them her dritten, her bitten, her koat, her skunkephant, her squippy, or any of her other mixed-up animals. Instead, she fluxed into her very best kitten, the one she could now hold for up to fifteen minutes without going wonky.

The teachers inspected Kitten-Nory, checking her whiskers and tail, and asked to see some of Nory's kittenball skills. Kittenball was like soccer, but played by kittens and with balls of yarn instead of balls. Kitten-Nory tail-whacked and batted, yaggled and pounced.

Then the teachers asked if she could do other animals. Most ten-year-old Fluxers would have said no. Advanced kids might have nervously volunteered to do puppy or hamster.

Nory politely asked for a fish tank and a towel.

When those arrived, she showed the examiners her puffer fish.

True, Puffer-Fish-Nory was tempted to go wonky in the tank. Sometimes it was very hard not to let her magic go upside down. But she popped back to girl form before anything went wrong. She climbed out of the tank and dried herself with the towel.

The teachers clapped. They actually clapped!

"Fish fluxing in fifth grade!" one of them said to Father. "Impressive!"

"Thank you," said Father, as if *he* was the one who had done puffer fish.

The examiners then asked for more animals. "If you have them, that is."

Nory wasn't sure what to do. Maybe she wouldn't go wonky if she fluxed very quickly?

She showed them puppy (for five seconds), goat (for five seconds), and mosquito (for five seconds).

The mosquito got them on their feet. A standing ovation.

"I have never seen a middle-school student do an insect," said the fluxing teacher. "Not in all my born days."

"Thank you," said Father again.

Nory knew that her mosquito had actually had a fuzzy kitten tail. The teachers just hadn't been able to see it. She had buzzed by them and quickly fluxed back into Girl-Nory.

And then, *phew*. The exam was over.

Afterward, Nory sat outside on a wooden bench in the entryway. She read a book. She watched the clock hands go around.

When she had *flunked* the Big Test, the answer had been clear right away: "Nosirree, we do not want you and your chaotic upside-down magic here at Sage."

But now, although they knew she was upside down, the teachers had also seen that she had a lot of power. Would they want her?

Did she want them to want her? She did want to be accepted. She wanted to be good enough. And she wanted to please Father, after disappointing him over and over. But she didn't want to leave Dunwiddle. Or her friends. Or her Upside-Down Magic class.

She waited.

And waited.

Apparently, there was quite a lot to discuss, because it was nearly forty-five minutes before Father walked out of the Hall of Magic and Performance to shake her hand.

"Congratulations, darling daughter!" he told Nory, grinning. "You've been admitted to Sage Academy. You'll begin after the winter holidays."

Wow.

Just wow.

Father had never called Nory "darling daughter" before. Like, ever.

But was she really going to leave Dunwiddle Magic School?

2

Outside Ms. Starr's classroom on Friday morning, a wonderful, terrible storm was brewing, and Elliott found it thrilling. Gray winter rain pelted the windows. Dark clouds rumbled and tumbled. Lately, Elliott's life had been feeling a bit dull. Predictable. He longed for something unexpected to happen, and this wild storm was a start.

He leaned over his desk and elbowed Nory. He was supposed to be doing silent seatwork with the other seven kids in the Upside-Down Magic class, but their teacher, Ms. Starr, had stepped out for a moment.

"Do you like the sound of rain as much as I do?"

Nory blinked. "Huh?"

"It's amazing, don't you think?"

"Whatever."

Hmm. Usually, Nory would have at least *looked* at the clouds. And probably gotten excited about them, too.

"Nory, is something wrong?" Elliott asked.

"Nah," Nory said. Then she sniffed and dragged the back of her hand under her nose. "Actually, *yes*. Did you know that I went to Sage yesterday? *All* the way there and *all* the way back?"

"What? Why?"

Just then, Ms. Starr came back into the classroom with a stack of papers. "I've got the handouts on baby ospreys!" she said. "Pepper, can you pass them out, please?"

Pepper went from row to row. Bax Kapoor took his handout and made it into a paper airplane. Bax was an Upside-Down Fluxer whose go-to fluxing animal was a rock. Which wasn't an animal.

Willa Ingeborg took her handout and began doodling on it. Technically, Willa was an Upside-Down Flare, because instead of making fire, she made rain. She didn't think that label accurately described her, so recently, she'd started calling herself a Fluid.

Elliott brought his attention back to Nory. He leaned over. "Why'd you go to Sage? Is your dad sick? Or Hawthorn or Dalia?"

"No, everyone's fine," Nory said.

"Then what happened?"

"Elliott," interrupted Ms. Starr. "Please pay attention. Why were the ospreys upset in the Grand Osprey Rebellion of 2012?"

"I don't know," said Elliott, embarrassed.

"The baby osprey . . . ?" hinted Ms. Starr. "His love of almonds . . . ?"

"Um, he really loved almonds?" Elliott tried.

Ms. Starr sighed and put aside her printout. "The storm's making it hard to focus, isn't it? Perhaps that's enough history for today. Let's use our last few minutes before lunch for interpretive dance."

She put on the UDM kids' new favorite song, "Don't Eat Paste," and let them dance until the bell rang.

The rain came down harder during lunch, lashing the wide cafeteria windows. Flashes of lightning made everyone's faces turn temporarily spooky. Elliott looked for Nory in the lunch line. He wanted to know what was wrong. But she wasn't in sight, so he waited by himself and got a huge blob of nasty-looking meat loaf and a smallish plop of mashed potatoes.

"Meat loaf again," moaned Bax when Elliott sat down. "It's too gross to eat. Do they want me to starve?"

Marigold Ramos joined them. No one quite knew what to call Marigold's magic. She wasn't an Upside-Down Flare, or Flicker, or anything else. What Marigold did was shrink things—and make them grow. Marigold herself liked to say she was a Fitter, but she'd made that up.

"I can help," Marigold told Bax. She shrank the

nasty meat loaf and bigged up the mashed potatoes. "Better?"

Bax made a sound that might have been "thank you." It was hard to tell, since his mouth was crammed with mashed potatoes.

Andres Padillo floated above them, eating the lunch he'd brought from home. Andres was an Upside-Down Flyer. He could fly *up* with no trouble; he just couldn't come back *down*. To sit at a desk like the other kids, he had to wear a backpack filled with bricks, but he often shrugged it off during lunch.

Pepper, Willa, and Sebastian sat down with their trays. Sebastian Boondoggle's upside-down magic allowed him to see invisible things, like radio waves and farts. He wore large dark aviator goggles every day to limit his vision and make his life easier.

Elliott scanned the room. "Where's Nory?" he asked.

"I'm here," Nory said, trudging toward them. On her tray was a grape. One single, measly grape.

"Is that all you're eating?" Andres called down from the ceiling.

Nory sighed. "I couldn't face the meat loaf." She sat down and poked her grape with her fork.

"Nory?" Elliott said. "Talk."

Nory bit her lip.

The other UDM kids fell silent.

"I sort of . . . well . . . I got admitted to Sage Academy," Nory mumbled, not meeting anyone's gaze.

"What?!" Elliott cried.

"No!" wailed Pepper. "Are you serious? How?"

Glumly, Nory told them the whole story. "I don't want to go," she said. "It's *my* life! But Father says I have to *get the highest-quality education*, whether I want to or not!"

"We'll definitely miss you," Elliott said slowly. "But it's cool that you got in." He didn't want Nory to leave Dunwiddle, but he wanted to cheer her up. "When do you start?"

"In January," Nory said. "At the beginning of the new semester."

"You can't leave, Nory," said Pepper. "What about us? And Coach, and Ms. Starr?"

Nory gazed at her helplessly. "I'm a kid. My dad's . . . you know what he's like. Aunt Margo's flying me back to Sage after school today. My dad planned an official orientation over the weekend."

"Okay, listen," Elliott said. "Maybe your dad will change his mind. Maybe you won't have to go! Anything can happen, right? But in the meantime, congratulations. Seriously. Just getting in is a big deal."

"Congratulations for what?" said someone from behind the table. "What's a big deal?"

Elliott glanced over his shoulder and saw a short girl with short blond hair. It was Lacey Clench, a Flare of average talent.

Back in ordinary school, Lacey and Elliott had been friends, along with some other kids who also turned out to have flare magic. They called themselves the

Sparkies. Then, when Elliott's upside-down magic bubbled up, Lacey and the others had labeled Elliott a "wonko" and unfriended him.

At the time, the rejection had really hurt. Sometimes it still did.

But these days, Elliott had new friends. Better friends.

"A spot at Sage opened for next semester, and Nory got it," Marigold told Lacey.

Lacey's chest rose and fell. "Nory got accepted to Sage? *Nory?!*"

"This is the point in the conversation when a nice person would tell Nory congratulations," Elliott said. He frowned. "Except, oh yeah—you're not nice. And oh yeah again—you also applied to Sage for this school year, didn't you, Lacey? But you didn't get in."

"Ouch," said Bax.

"Shut up, Elliott," Lacey said. "You know nothing about it, and anyway, I know you're lying! If there was an opening at Sage Academy, it would be mine.

I'm at the top of the wait list! My dad told me. I could get in at any minute."

Crash! A chunk of plaster banged onto a nearby table. Kids screamed and drew back.

"OMG," Lacey said. "What did you wonkos do now?"

"What?" Elliott said. "We didn't do anything!"

"Then why is the ceiling coming down?" Lacey demanded.

The ceiling tiles shook. The lights blinked and buzzed. Five square feet of plaster, paint, and paste crashed to the center of the UDM table, followed by a flood of water.

3

School ended early. The building flooded and had to be evacuated. And still, it kept raining.

Aunt Margo drove Nory to Sage instead of flying her there. Otherwise it would have been an extremely wet trip.

"Stone wants you to stay for the weekend, so I'll pick you up on Sunday night," she told Nory when they arrived at Sage Academy. Stone was Nory's father's first name. It suited him. "Try to have fun, kiddo. Okay?"

"I'll try." She hugged Aunt Margo goodbye, grabbed her bag, and hurried through the rain to the administration building. She found Father waiting in the lobby. His coat and umbrella were a dignified gray. He handed Nory an umbrella in the same color.

"Let's walk through campus," he said jovially. Father was *never* jovial. "I want to show you our newest dormitory, as well as the building designated for our Fluxers. I've got quite a lot of Sage Academy history to share with you!"

Nory and Father walked beneath their umbrellas to a large brick building that looked more modern than the rest of the campus. It was the new dorm. Most students at Sage lived on campus, though there were a few day students, like Dalia and Hawthorn.

The new dorm was fancy, with arched ceilings and decorative moldings. Father pointed out the architectural features and explained something about how an older dormitory was scheduled for demolition, but Nory didn't pay much attention. She had other things on her mind.

Elliott had said it was a big deal to get into Sage. And he was right. She knew he was.

Plus, Father was so very pleased.

But.

Sage Academy.

As Nory trailed behind Father, she felt anxious in the presence of all this grandeur, all this pressure, the uniforms and the rules. She loved Dunwiddle Magic School. Could she possibly be happy here at Sage? With so many decorative moldings?

Father lectured Nory about the many famous magicians who had attended Sage. He talked about the importance of tradition, citing rituals like the Spring Unicorn Festival and the annual school-wide game of hide-and-seek, which students and teachers alike took part in every winter. He talked about recent sports victories and magic electives and student affinity groups.

Nory knew Sage Academy had a lot to offer! She just couldn't imagine feeling at home here. The sad truth was that this was Father's place, and she never quite felt at home with him.

When the tour ended, Father invited Nory to come wait at his office until the end of the school day, when together they could go home and join Dalia and Hawthorn for a family dinner. He introduced Nory to his administrative secretary, who was tapping at her computer while in the shape of a capuchin monkey.

"Sorry!" she said, changing back into human form. "I fluxed on my coffee break and forgot to switch back!"

"Please remember that only certain animal forms are acceptable for work, Ms. Fujita," reprimanded Father. "Your monkey tends to be . . . messy. We want to command respect at all times, yes?"

"Yes," said Ms. Fujita. "I'll stick to horse and leopard."

"Thank you."

At five thirty, Father's computer rang, indicating a video call.

"Hmm," said Father. He squinted at the monitor. "It's Principal Gonzalez. Now, why is he calling?

I haven't told him about your acceptance to Sage Academy yet. I really don't know what this could be about."

Principal Gonzalez was the head of Dunwiddle Magic School. He and Father weren't exactly friends. In fact, they were more like rivals.

The computer trilled again. Reluctantly, Father jabbed at the keyboard. "Feliciano," he said. "How are you?"

"Hello, Stone," said Principal Gonzalez. "I need your help."

Father, who was a powerful Flicker, made the old coffee mug on his desk disappear. "Oh?"

"We've had a flood here. Some pipes were rusty, and it seems they broke. It's quite a mess, to be honest."

The filing cabinet behind Father's chair disappeared. "We don't allow rust at Sage Academy," he said. "Our pipes are examined annually."

"My school is a danger zone," Principal Gonzalez continued. "We can't return to the building until repairs are done, so we're farming out our students to nearby schools. My eighth-grade Flickers are going to school in Cider Cup, my seventh-grade Flares are going to Frostville, and so on."

Father noticed a stain on the front of his shirt. He put his hand to his mouth, then made *himself* invisible.

"Stone?" said Principal Gonzalez.

"I'm here."

"I haven't found a school to take my fifth-grade Flares, nor the eight children in the Upside-Down Magic class. And since your daughter is one of the students who needs a space, I thought you might be willing to host my students for one week. We cannot pay tuition, of course." He coughed. "I'm asking you for a favor."

Nory edged out of her chair. The Upside-Down Magic class, here at Sage next week? Along with the fifth-grade Flares?

She sidled closer. She wasn't sure she wanted

everybody here, in her hometown, at Father's school. Father hated wonky magic. It made him uptight. And some of her friends were accident-prone. Willa might flood the classrooms. Marigold might shrink someone by accident. Pepper would definitely scare the animals in the Fuzzy lab.

What if Father yelled at them? Or gave them time-outs?

On the other hand, Principal Gonzalez sounded desperate. And Nory wanted her friends to have *somewhere* to go.

She approached the chair where she assumed her dad was still sitting. "Please say yes," she whispered. "They really need your help!"

"Is that Nory?" asked Principal Gonzalez. She leaned in and waved at him on the video chat. He smiled, making his enormous mustache twitch.

"Fine," said Father, still invisible.

"What?" Principal Gonzalez's eyes widened. "Did you just say yes?"

"Against my better judgment, I did," said Father. "The students in question can arrive Sunday night. I will have Ms. Fujita call you with the details. We'll issue them uniforms. You're welcome—and goodbye."

4

On Sunday evening, Elliott climbed aboard Dunwiddle's yellow school bus with the other UDM kids (except Nory), the fifth-grade Flares, and Nurse Riley. The engine rumbled to life, and they were off.

I can't believe it, Elliott thought. *Me! At Sage Academy!* Some of his friends were anxious about being shipped off to the fanciest of the fancy private schools, but Elliott saw it as an adventure.

Andres was excited, too. He sat next to Elliott, wearing his brickpack, and bounced on the scratched-up seat. "I can't wait to see Tip," Andres said. "And Phoebe! And Lark and Tomás!"

The UDM kids had met some Sage kids before, when fifth graders from both schools had attended an overnight field trip at a dragon rescue center. Andres had bonded with several of the Flyers.

Elliott looked around. He leaned forward and tapped Marigold. "Where's Willa?"

"She's not coming," Marigold said over her shoulder. "She has the flu."

"She wasn't sick on Friday," Elliott said.

"She's faking," Bax said.

"Why would she do that?" Marigold asked.

"Um, maybe because she's afraid of raining all over the school and ruining the ancient tapestries and the velvet curtains?" Bax said.

The UDM kids went quiet.

"What if I accidentally *shrink* the velvet curtains?" Marigold said in a small voice.

"You won't," Elliott insisted. "No way." *And no way will I freeze them, either,* he told himself.

He could hear the Sparkies' shrill laughter from the front of the bus. That was the only part of this adventure he wasn't up for. Traveling with the Sparkies. Why had the UDM kids been paired with the Flares? Why couldn't they have gone to Sage with the fifth-grade Fuzzies? He made a tiny ice cube in his hand and popped it in his mouth.

"Oh, nice," Andres said. He pulled a grape juice box from the zippered pocket of his brickpack and tossed it to Elliott. "Make me a Popsicle?"

Elliott froze the juice box.

"Pass it here, and I'll big it up," Marigold said. "Then we can share." She bigged the frozen juice box to be the size of a cereal box.

Andres used his pen cap to slice open the box and then broke the massive grape ice cube into shareable pieces.

Everyone sucked on their chunks. Their mouths turned purple.

"Ms. Starr is meeting us there, right?" Elliott asked. "Maybe she's riding with Mr. Zlotnick." Mr. Zlotnick taught the typical Flare students, and he wasn't on the bus either. The only Dunwiddle staff person was Nurse Riley, who was sitting in the front row, talking to the bus driver.

"She better be," Marigold said, talking about Ms. Starr. "How would we have class without her?"

After a two-hour drive, the bus stopped in front of a large gold gate.

Whoa. Fancy.

The driver checked in with a uniformed security guard and the gates swung open.

Everyone peered out the windows as they drove down the road to the lit-up buildings ahead of them. There were at least fifteen different buildings, all made of stone.

"It's like a village," Marigold whispered.

"All of this is part of the Sage campus?" Andres asked. "*All* of it?"

"All of this and more," said Lacey from up front.

"They have different buildings for different magical subjects, and a separate gymnasium building, a separate auditorium, a dining hall, and dormitories. I know from going on the tour."

A building for each magical talent? Wow. Would there be a building for upside-down magic?

The bus driver stopped and a small brown horse trotted toward the bus. The bus door hissed open, and the horse fluxed into a woman, who stepped gracefully aboard.

"Good evening," she said. "I'm Ms. Fujita, Dr. Horace's assistant. I'm here to show you to the Buxbom Dorm, where you will be staying while you're visiting." She turned to the driver. "Continue straight ahead and make a right."

The bus driver followed her directions.

"Keep going," Ms. Fujita said. "Yes, yes, keep going."

The road curved around. Elliott spotted three goats, trotting along together with backpacks in their mouths. They must be fluxed students.

After the bus passed two more buildings, Ms. Fujita asked the driver to stop.

"Here we are," she said as everyone disembarked. "My apologies for the state of the dorm. It's due to be demolished! Next month! But we weren't expecting guests, and these are our only available beds, and—well!" She smiled. "What good timing, after all."

"Not a problem," Nurse Riley said. "We appreciate you taking us in. Come on, kids. Grab your bags and—"

"Our grounds crew will get your bags," Ms. Fujita said. "Go on to your rooms. I'm sure you're tired! We've put your names on your doors. Your uniforms are in your closets."

"This is the *old* dorm?" said Bax, walking ahead. "I don't get what's wrong with it."

"The new dorm must be a palace," said Pepper.

The entryway had deep red carpet and vaulted ceilings. Farther on was a common area furnished with stately leather couches, more thick carpets, and a number of glossy wooden tables. Bookshelves were loaded with a mix of paperbacks and textbooks. Elliott had never seen such a fancy space meant for *kids*.

He found his room and stood in its center, taking it in. The walls were papered with a rich blue-and-gold floral pattern. The furniture was simple: a bed, a wooden desk, a swivel chair. He had a big window with, yes, blue velvet curtains, and a closet that contained five days' worth of school uniforms.

Down the hall were the bathrooms. There, Elliott could see that the building was past its prime. The porcelain sinks were stained with use, the tiles warped and cracked with age.

He went back out to the common room and found Pepper on one of the leather couches.

"Have you seen Nory?" he asked.

"Elinor Horace will not be staying in the dormitory," said Ms. Fujita, appearing behind them and making Elliott jump. "She will remain at her father's house."

"Oh," he said. "How come?"

"Dr. Horace's wishes."

"What about Ms. Starr?" Pepper asked. "Is she staying with us or in, like, a teachers' dorm?"

"Ms. Starr?" Ms. Fujita repeated.

"Our teacher."

Ms. Fujita frowned. "I was told that your school nurse would be your chaperone. He'll be sleeping in the prefect room."

"I don't understand," Elliott said.

"Yeah," said Pepper. "Who's going to teach us if our teacher isn't here?"

"You'll attend classes with the Sage students, of course," Ms. Fujita said.

"Wait," Elliott said, his heart sinking. "That's fine for the Flares, maybe. But what about the kids with Upside-Down Magic?"

"Sage doesn't have an Upside-Down Magic class," Ms. Fujita explained. "You'll be grouped by your magic: Flare, Fuzzy, Flyer, Fluxer, or Flicker."

Elliott's jaw dropped. "But . . . I freeze things!"

Pepper laughed nervously. "And I can't go to a

Fuzzy class. I'll terrify all the animals! Is that what Sage wants? A stampede of terrified kittens?"

By this time, other students had come into the common room: Sebastian, Andres, and Marigold, plus Lacey, Rune, and some other Flares.

"I'm sure it will be fine," said Ms. Fujita.

"I'm pretty sure it won't," said Pepper.

"No kidding!" said Lacey. She turned to Rune and laughed. "They're setting the wonkos free. Did you hear?"

Elliott felt sick. He would have to be in a class with Lacey. And all the Sparkies. And since Willa had the "flu," he'd have to deal with them all on his own.

5

At Sage, every school day started with morning assembly. Nory, foolishly, expected it to be fun. Father had said it was his favorite part of the day, and Nory had imagined clowns and seals parading up and down the grand rows of the Hall of Magic and Performance. Also doughnuts.

Guess how many clowns and seals there were?

Zero.

Guess how many doughnuts?

Also zero.

Instead, a teacher scolded at Nory for having her sleeves rolled up, and all the students had to listen to a chamber music quartet.

Pepper squeezed her hand as they sat on the purple velvet seats. Nory squeezed back. She was worried about herself and Bax in the Fluxer class. And she knew she'd miss Ms. Starr. She could only imagine how Pepper felt about joining the Fuzzy class.

"We missed you in the dorm," Pepper whispered.

"My dad wouldn't let me come," Nory said. "I wanted to."

A Sage teacher whipped around from the pew in front of them. "Shh!"

Finally, assembly was over. The students were dismissed and broke into chatter.

"Hey, look!" Pepper said.

Nory looked and—

"Mitali!" she exclaimed, calling out to a girl with bright eyes, a big smile, light brown skin, and dark brown hair cut in a swingy bob.

"Nory!" cried Mitali, pushing through the throng.

Nory had met Mitali at Dragon Haven. They had formed a friendship almost immediately.

"I am so happy to see you!" said Mitali. "Omigosh, we're going to have so much fun. How do you like the uniform?"

Nory waved goodbye to Pepper, promising to catch up with her at lunch, and hoped that the day would get better.

It did!

Nory knew several other Sage Fluxers from Dragon Haven, not just Mitali: Fuchsia, Anemone, and Fred. And they were all glad to see her!

Plus, they were nice to Bax! And Bax was nice to them!

Math wasn't too hard. And literature was actually interesting. They read a short story about a unicorn-fluxing princess.

Third period was fluxing class. The teacher was

a tall man with a giraffe-like neck and a kind smile. His name was Mr. Lan.

"You're Stone Horace's daughter, yes?" he said to Nory.

She nodded.

"I've heard a lot about you," said Mr. Lan. "All good. Don't worry."

Nory wasn't sure she believed him, but she wanted to.

Mr. Lan did a presentation about canine fluxing, talking about techniques for holding on to the human mind and ways of relating to actual dogs when in dog form. The Sage Fluxers were ahead of the Dunwiddle Fluxers. That's why they were working on puppies instead of kittens.

Uh-oh. Nory was great at kitten, but her puppy went wonky almost every time she'd done it. She really didn't want to go unintentionally upside down on her first day at Sage.

She tried to do the deep breathing Ms. Starr had

taught her. The other students demonstrated their homework by fluxing into pug, golden retriever, dalmatian, and beagle puppies. Then Mr. Lan beckoned Nory to the front of the room. "Would you show us your puppy, please? Any breed is fine."

Nory took another deep breath. She reminded herself that she'd done puppy in the entrance exam. Sure, it had only been for five seconds, but she'd done it. She could do it again.

Pop pop pop! She fluxed into a golden retriever puppy.

"Very nice," Puppy-Nory heard Mr. Lan say. "Perfectly floppy puppy ears. Top-notch fluxing!"

Puppy-Nory wagged her tail. She was holding it! It was six seconds at least! Last time Nory had done puppy, she'd added in squid tentacles. But no squid today. No way was she even going to think about squids!

Squids. Squids. Squids. Now that she had thought of them, Puppy-Nory couldn't stop thinking of them.

No, Puppy-Nory told herself, holding on to her human self with all her might.

She wiggled one of her front paws. *Eeek!* She felt a tentacle wanting to burst through.

She wiggled one of her back paws. *Ack!* Another tentacle tried to push out. Puppy-Nory only barely managed to keep it in!

She wagged her tail, and—uh-oh. A *huge* tentacle wanted *hugely* to slither out, and no no no!

Hold your tail still! Puppy-Nory told herself, focusing all her might on keeping control of her human mind. *Hold! Your! Tail! Still!*

Plink!

Puppy-Nory held her tail still. Only it wasn't a puppy tail anymore. Or a squid tentacle. It was an elephant tail.

And then, *plunk*! Her puppy ears grew and stretched and waggled back and forth like satellites.

"Elephant ears!" cried Fred.

"So cool!" cried Anemone.

"Nory, you're an elephant-puppy!" said Mitali.

"An elepup!" said Fuchsia.

"No, a puppephant!" said Anemone.

Mr. Lan cleared his throat. "Elinor. Flux back, please."

Nory did. *Pop!* She was a girl again.

"Well. That was not uninteresting," Mr. Lan said.

Nory was frustrated at having gone wonky. She wanted to *choose* when she fluxed into unusual animals and when she didn't. But she was also a bit proud of her puppephant. She had never done that particular upside-down creature before. It seemed full of possibility. Plus, her Fluxer friends were beaming at her. Well, except for Bax. Bax wasn't a beamer.

"But it was *not* a puppy," continued Mr. Lan.

"It was better than a puppy!" cried Mitali.

"I want you to work on puppy and puppy only," Mr. Lan told Nory. "At Sage, if I ask for puppy, I expect puppy. Is that clear?"

Nory nodded glumly. Coach, her fluxing tutor, would have asked her to do puppephant again, right away. He would have wanted to help her learn how to do it at will.

"Also, your shirt is untucked," Mr. Lan pointed out. "And there is something sticky on the side of your mouth. At Sage, we pay attention to personal hygiene."

Mitali smiled at Nory sympathetically, which helped a little. But mainly Nory felt like a deflated balloon.

"Moving on." Mr. Lan focused on Bax. "Bax Kapoor, is it? Puppy, please."

"I can't," said Bax.

"I'm sorry?" Mr. Lan replied.

"You and me both," said Bax.

Mr. Lan frowned. "You are a Fluxer," he stated.

"I guess."

"Then flux. Flux into whatever you can manage!"

With a sigh, Bax fluxed into a player piano and played a jaunty trill. The Sage kids oohed and aahed.

Mr. Lan did not. "Good heavens, flux back."

"He can't," Nory said.

Player-Piano-Bax played a dramatic succession of chords to underscore her words, *dum dum DUM*.

"He has to go to the nurse," Nory went on to explain. "Nurse Riley. He came from Dunwiddle with us?"

Player-Piano-Bax played the opening melody of Scott Joplin's "The Entertainer," bouncing on his wooden piano legs.

"Enough!" said Mr. Lan to Player-Piano-Bax. He raised his voice. "Go get Nurse Riley!"

Sigh.

Earlier in the day, hanging out with Mitali, Nory had thought she had a chance of fitting in at Sage Academy. Perhaps. Maybe.

Now it didn't look likely at all.

6

Elliott got stuck in the same class as Lacey and Rune. He and the thirty Dunwiddle Flares were divided into two groups, joining up with two Sage flaring classes. Elliott's group went straight to Flare Studies, while the other class went to science.

The Flare Studies building was surrounded by a moat, for fire protection. Inside, there were the usual fire extinguishers everywhere, but the classroom was also completely lined in a rubbery fire-protectant material. Fancy!

The teacher, Dr. Vogel, was a round lady with her hair scraped back in a tight bun. She wore a pantsuit and large tortoiseshell glasses, and she seemed dismayed to see the sixteen Dunwiddle kids.

"Here at Sage we pride ourselves on having very small groups of students," she said to Ms. Fujita. She didn't even lower her voice. "I don't think we are meeting that part of our mission if I double my class size."

"Dr. Horace said you're to take them," said Ms. Fujita. She gave a little squeak, turned into a leopard, and bounded off.

Dr. Vogel sighed and clapped her hands for the students' attention. "Dunwiddle Flares!" she exclaimed sharply.

What? Oh, no.

"It seems no one told you that the tie is mandatory," said Dr. Vogel. She evil-eyed Lacey until Lacey gulped, fished her tie out of her pocket, and put it on. It was a clip-on, at least.

Then Dr. Vogel pursed her lips and blew a thin stream of fire out of her mouth, as if she were whistling.

"Today we're going to practice fire breathing," she said. "It may be new to a number of you."

Elliott's dad was a Flare, so Elliott had seen a good amount of flaring, but his dad didn't do anything very difficult. There *was* fancy flaring on TV, of course, but it was different seeing the teacher breathing fire, live.

Next, Dr. Vogel gave each student a device that looked like a magnifying glass, but without any glass in it. She called them "circlometers."

"We're developing fire-breathing strength as a way to help your overall flame intensity," she said. "Though most of our flare magic comes from our hands, fire breathing increases our overall flaring strength. It's a helpful warm-up exercise. Breathe fire and you flare better, even if your fire breaths are small."

Elliott had never breathed fire. In fact, he hardly ever flared, period. When his magic first came in, his flames had always fizzled quickly, and ice had come out instead.

He hadn't even tried to flare since September, when Ms. Starr had convinced him to focus on his ice power, since it was so much stronger than his fire power.

Elliott closed his eyes and tried to feel his inner flame.

It *was* there—feeble, but there—only as soon as he sensed it, his ice magic took over and froze it. His "iciness" seemed to pool most strongly in his wrists, so he rotated them in both directions, trying to shake free any possible blockage.

"How's it going, Ice Boy?" Rune taunted.

"Aw, don't be mean," said Lacey. "We shouldn't pick on people who are incredibly awkward and bad at school."

Just because I used to be friends with you at ordinary school doesn't mean I care what you think now, thought Elliott. *I don't care. I'm glad to be a Freezer and my parents support me and I won't let you Sparkies spoil my day.*

He told himself all that, but his hands still trembled.

Dr. Vogel asked everyone to try blowing a very small, very short puff of flame through the circle of their circlometers.

Poof! Most of the Sage Flares blew puffs.

Poof! Some of the Dunwiddle Flares blew puffs.

Poof! Rune blew a puff.

Piff! Lacey blew, but no puff came out.

Ha!

Dr. Vogel loomed over Elliott. "Elliott? Why are you not poofing your puff? I do not require that you succeed, but I do require that you try."

The room went quiet. Everyone stopped trying to poof puffs and stared at Elliott.

"He has super-weak fire," explained Rune.

"Yeah, he can only make, like, the weakest little

sad spark," added Lacey. "We all feel very sorry for him, all the time."

"Elliott's got the upside-down magic problem," Rune whispered. "He's not even allowed to be in our regular classes, back home."

Elliott could hear murmurings of the Sage Flares as they absorbed that info and passed it along.

"Try, Elliott!" insisted Dr. Vogel. "Ignore the titterings of your fellow students. Their manners are atrocious."

The teacher had taken his side! Elliott glanced at Lacey. Her hands were in her lap and she was looking at them very intently.

He looked for the fire inside. He found nothing, so he brought nothing up to his throat. He breathed in, as the teacher had instructed, and—

Preeff! His breath covered the circlometer with tiny, beautiful shapes of frost and then completely iced it over. Elliott dropped it on the desk, and the ice shattered. Shards fell on the floor and on his desk.

Suddenly, all the Sage Flares and most of the Dunwiddle Flares were standing around Elliott. Staring. Pointing.

"What did he do?"

"He iced it."

"I never heard of anyone *icing* anything."

"Well, he iced it anyway."

"That's super weird."

"Is he okay?"

"Elliott, are you okay?"

"Maybe he should go to the nurse."

"Do you want someone to take you to the nurse, Elliott?"

A lot of the kids were being nice, actually, even if they did think he must be sick.

Dr. Vogel patted Elliott on the shoulder and said, "Thank you for trying. Please continue to try every single exercise I give. Do you understand?"

"Okay," said Elliott. He just wanted to go home. Home to his parents, who saved his best ice objects in the freezer. Home to his baby brother, who ran to him the minute he got home from school, every single day.

"You say, *I understand, Dr. Vogel*," the teacher corrected him.

"I understand, Dr. Vogel," said Elliott.

7

After the puppephant and the player piano, and after taking Bax to see Nurse Riley, Nory had felt miserable. She stayed miserable for an entire hour, but now she was determined to look on the bright side.

Everything would be fine!

It would be great!

After all, she had friends at Sage. The monkey gymnasium would be cool, once she learned monkey fluxing. She was making Father happy.

Oh, and the campus was pretty.

Yes, the campus sure was pretty.

She would focus her thoughts on that pretty campus.

At lunchtime, she filled out school paperwork with Father. Then she scurried to the cafeteria to sit down with the UDM kids, but they were mostly packing up. She scarfed her milk and pasta, then dashed off to more classes.

The school day finally ended, and Nory and Bax hurried to the Alderwood Lounge to meet the others.

The lounge had several couches, velvet curtains (zamboozle, this school was obsessed with velvet!), some vending machines, a few red beanbags, and a foosball table. Elliott and Sebastian sat on a couch, sharing a bag of Wild Potato Hots and drinking apple juice. Marigold was bigging up the beanbags so they were ridiculously large and comfy-looking. Andres bobbed on the ceiling.

"How are you doing?" Nory asked everyone as

she and Bax plopped into the bigged-up beanbags. "Did you love the rest of your day?"

She wanted them to love it. After all, *she* was determined to love it.

"The campus is pretty," Marigold said.

"Yes!" cried Nory. "Exactly!"

"And big!" Andres said. "So big. So much walking outside."

"Who held your leash?" Elliott asked. "Or did you have to wear your brickpack all day?" He tilted up his head to better see Andres.

"Tip held it," Andres said. "He didn't mind."

"Did I tell you they put me with Sebastian and the Flickers?" Marigold asked.

"No way," Nory said.

"That class has less students, so that's where they decided to put me. It was fine," Marigold reported. "We spent most of class playing checkers. Everyone got a board, and they were supposed to make either all the red squares or all the black squares invisible. I just practiced shrinking the whole board and bigging it up again. The teacher didn't seem to care as long as I didn't get in the way. And Sebastian—" She burst out laughing. "Sebastian, tell them what happened at Invisible Diving!"

"You went to the pool?" Nory asked.

"Yes!" Marigold said. "In Flicker gym. Sebastian and I had to go even though we can't make ourselves invisible. We all had to wear green bathing suits."

"Isn't the pool pretty?" Nory asked. "So very pretty."

"Tell them what happened, Sebastian!" Marigold said.

"Well," Sebastian said, adjusting his aviator goggles, "I could see the divers. When they're invisible. And one of them—"

"The tall redhead! Miller! With the bushy eyebrows!" Marigold added.

"He, ah, relieved himself in the pool."

"You saw him peeing underwater?" Andres asked. "But peeing's not a sound."

"Urination is actually a very intense sound," Sebastian answered. "Bright yellow. I could see it from all the way at the back of the diving board line."

"Did you say anything to him?" Nory asked.

"I just announced to the Flickers that I could see the sounds of urination. And farts. I added the farts in so as not to be obvious."

"Miller turned bright red!" Marigold said.

"How was your day, Elliott?" Nory knew he'd had the worst luck of all of them, being stuck with the Sparkies.

Elliott sighed. "The magic lessons were tough," he admitted. "Lacey made fun of me and made sure everyone knew my magic was wonky."

"I'm sorry," Nory said. "Lacey's the worst. But what about last night? Did you have fun, sleeping in the dorms?"

"I was a little homesick," said Andres.

"I was homesick, too," said Pepper, plopping down on a huge beanbag. "And I don't think the Fuzzies were that happy to have me around today. We went to the rare animals room, which had a rhino and a black unicorn and some dragons."

"Wow!" said Marigold.

"The unicorn started shrieking when I walked in, so I had to wait outside. Then we went to the skunk garden, and guess what? They made me stay outside *again*. They were afraid of all the skunks spraying at once and stinking up the campus. Did any of you get to see it? Apparently, they use it for eighth-grade exams—you flunk if you get sprayed."

They all shook their heads.

"The teacher said I should probably just hang out in the library tomorrow," Pepper said, sighing.

"I was forced to turn into a piano and spent most of the day with Nurse Riley," Bax said.

Nory hated that her friends weren't all happy. If they loved Sage, maybe Nory could love it, too. She needed to lift their spirits. She started to sing their new favorite song—"Don't Eat Paste"—quietly at first. Then louder.

Don't eat paste
But do eat butter
Don't borrow money
But call your mother

She was off-key—Nory was always off-key! But she sang loudly and was happy to see Pepper begin doing percussion, drumming on her shoulders and knees.

Elliott joined in to harmonize on "borrow money," and even Bax's foot was tapping.

You think there are rules
But there are none none none
You think there are rules
But you've already won
I won't break (ake ake ake)
Don't mistake (ake ake ake)

Now Bax was singing, too, and Marigold was clapping her hands.

Nory had done it. She had cheered them up, and made herself feel hopeful in the process.

Sage would be good, wouldn't it? Mitali and puppy lessons and time with Hawthorn and Dalia.

> *Don't eat paste*
> *But do eat butter*
> *Don't borrow money*
> *But call your mother!*

"Dunwiddle students!" a grown-up voice snapped.

Nory looked up to see a stern-looking teacher glaring at them. "There are no loud voices allowed in the Alderwood Lounge! Study period is in session just across the hall!"

No lounging in the lounge? Was he kidding?

All the UDM kids sank into their seats.

"We'll be quieter," Nory whispered as her heart deflated. "I promise."

8

The next morning, Nory ate two sunny-side-up eggs that Hawthorn cooked for her. She wondered what her friends were eating in the cafeteria.

"Nory," Father said as he turned to leave the house, briefcase in hand. "I heard about what happened in the Alderwood Lounge. Follow the rules, please." Then he left.

"What happened in the lounge?" Dalia asked.

"Um . . . I sang?" Nory said. "With my friends."

"Yikes," Hawthorn said, eyes wide. "What did you sing?"

"'Don't Eat Paste.'"

"Seriously? While study period was going on?"

"It's all the way down the hall!"

"You're only supposed to sing in the choir room," Hawthorn warned her. "And in assembly, when it's time for the alma mater." He glanced at the clock. "Oh. Speaking of, we better get going!"

At assembly, Father lectured about classical music in the 1900s. He droned on and on and on.

Nory's eyes glazed over.

Her back hurt.

The lights were too bright.

She squirmed in her seat.

She accidentally elbowed Bax, who sat slumped over with his eyes closed, taking a nap.

At least she wasn't the only one who found this boring. Did her siblings really sit through this every morning?

Nory searched for Dalia and found her three rows up on the right side, but couldn't see her face. And Hawthorn? She twisted around to search for him. There he was! About ten rows back on the left side and—oh, wow, he was fully absorbed in the lecture. Weird!

Nory felt a tap on her knee. The Fluxer next to her—Anemone—pointed at a nearby teacher.

The teacher motioned Nory to sit forward in her seat and pay attention.

Nory sat forward. She paid attention.

"You have to apologize," whispered Anemone.

"Sorry," Nory mouthed. The teacher gave a sharp nod and glanced away.

Nory apologized again during first period, when she got in trouble for speaking without raising her hand.

Then again during second period, when she spent too long in the bathroom.

She wondered what she'd have to apologize for during third period.

In fluxing class, after Mr. Lan had instructed them to turn into puppies, he commanded them all to sit.

Sit.

Stand.

Sit.

Lie down.

Sit.

Stand.

Sit.

Lie down.

Mr. Lan drilled them again and again and again.

But Puppy-Nory didn't want to sit, stand, or lie down. Puppy-Nory wanted to fetch.

Ruff! Ruff! Ruff! She would fetch that shiny red thing on the table!

Puppy-Nory trotted over.

Yes, she had it! She was biting it by the handle.

Now where could she take it? Maybe outside? She could dig a hole and bury it.

"Nory!" Mr. Lan snapped. "Put my coffee mug back on my desk immediately. And please remember your human mind. It appears you have lost it."

RRRRroow! Puppy-Nory would not drop the shiny red thing.

"Pay attention, Nory. Don't flux back to human," said Mr. Lan. "The goal is to remain a puppy and regain control. Use the Pinkholder technique."

Puppy-Nory did not know what the Pinkholder technique was, but she did know when she was being scolded. She dropped the mug on the hard floor.

Crack! It shattered. Ceramic mug bits went everywhere.

Mr. Lan glared at her. "My daughter gave me that mug for Father's Day."

Pop!

Nory fluxed back into human form. She couldn't help it. "Oh, zwingo," she said. "I could glue it back together! Want me to glue it back together?"

"Don't bother," he said.

Nory's cheeks burned, and for the zillionth time, she apologized. "Sorry, Mr. Lan," she said. "I'll try harder. I promise."

At lunch, Nory heaved a sigh of relief when she sat down with her friends. "I don't know how much more of this I can take," she told Pepper. "Every other word out of my mouth is 'sorry.'"

"What do you mean?" Pepper asked.

"'Sorry I talked without raising my hand,' 'Sorry I took so long in the bathroom,' 'Sorry I broke your special Father's Day coffee mug—'"

"You what?" asked Marigold.

"She fetched it when she was a puppy," Bax explained. "It was kind of hilarious."

"Maybe for you!" Nory protested. "You're lucky you don't have to do anything! You just get to sit there watching me get in trouble."

"For once we agree," said Bax. "Watching you get in trouble is definitely amusing."

Nory bonked her head on the table. "Ugh, I miss Ms. Starr. Everything is so serious here. And formal. And strict. And—"

"You." An older Sage student loomed over them. She was tall and wore her black hair in a tight braid that went all the way down to her waist.

"Me?" Nory asked.

"You. I've been looking for you."

"Why?"

"I'm Monitor Sorbee. You see this table you're sitting at? How it goes all the way down the room?"

"Um, yes?"

"I sit at the other end of it. And monitor."

"Okay," Nory said.

"They told us to sit here," Elliott put in. "At our first meal. This is where they told us to sit."

"I am aware!" snapped Monitor Sorbee. She turned back to Nory. "When you don't throw out your garbage, the lunch patrol removes points on our table score. Do you know what we got this morning at breakfast?"

"I wasn't here for breakfast," Nory said.

"I am aware," said Sorbee. "And we got a ten. Do you know what we got at dinner last night?"

"I wasn't here for dinner either," Nory said.

"We got a ten then, too. And do you know what we got for lunch yesterday?"

"Another ten?"

"No. No, we did not. We got a nine point five. Our first nine point five since September eighteenth. Do you know why we got a nine point five instead of a ten?"

"I am not aware?" Nory said.

"We got a nine point five because somebody, and that somebody was you, left her empty milk carton on the table. I know it was you because I saw you drinking from that milk carton earlier."

"I put my plate in the wash bin," Nory said. "I thought I had tossed my milk carton."

"You didn't. But you better do it today. Are we clear?"

Nory nodded.

Sorbee stormed off, and Elliott put his hand on Nory's shoulder. "You okay?"

She nodded. But she wasn't. Not really.

9

F lare class was after lunch on Tuesdays. After
thirty minutes of fire-breathing practice, during which Elliott accidentally froze his tongue,
Dr. Vogel collected the circlometers. She asked how
their homework had gone. "Who was able to flare the
water to ninety-eight degrees in under five seconds?"

No one raised a hand.

"Under ten seconds?"

Five of the Sage students raised their hands.
When Lacey saw theirs, hers shot up as well.

"Under twenty seconds?"

The remaining Flares in the class raised their hands. Everyone except Elliott.

"Under thirty?" the teacher asked him.

He shook his head. "Ninety-seven seconds."

Rune and Lacey snickered.

"There is no reason to laugh," Dr. Vogel said. She strode to Elliott. "You did that by flaring? Not by cooling hot water?"

"Yes, Dr. Vogel. By flaring."

She nodded. "Well done. I bet the fire-breathing exercises are helping, even if you can't breathe fire. I want you to practice again tonight. Both the fire breathing and the water warming. I want you to see if you can do it in under seventy seconds."

Seventy? Elliott was never going to be able to do that. He had spent two hours trying to do it in under two minutes!

"Okay, everyone, take out your paper bull's-eyes," Dr. Vogel said. "We are going to hone our precision skills with target practice. Whoever burns the small-est hole through the exact center of the target will be awarded extra homework, just for fun!"

Everyone groaned.

Dr. Vogel smiled. "Or, if our winner prefers, they can burn their lowest quiz score, so to speak, as a way of raising their grade."

Everyone cheered.

"You didn't win at target practice," Lacey said to Elliott as they walked out of class. "Shock of the century, I know."

"Neither did you," Elliott retorted.

"At least I *burned* the target," Lacey said.

At least I'm a decent human being who doesn't make people feel bad on purpose, Elliott thought.

"You better get to work on that water warm-ing," Lacey said. "You're embarrassing the rest of us. We can't have Sage thinking all Dunwiddle kids are wonkos."

She flounced away, her blond bob swinging.

"Is she always so horrible?" a short boy with green braces asked.

"Yes," Elliott said. "In fact, she's just getting started."

"Maybe she's jealous," the boy said.

"Ha! No way."

"I'm serious," the boy said. "That ice trick you did yesterday was really cool."

"Thanks," Elliott said, surprised.

"I'm GJ, by the way. Can you make ice out of *anything*?" GJ asked.

"Most things. I make slushies and Popsicles out of juice."

"Dude!" GJ's face lit up. "Can you make us some tomorrow at lunch? I'll find the juice."

"For sure." Elliott grinned.

Nory didn't think she could mess up any more, but mess up she did.

She got scolded for having an ink stain on her shirt in geography.

She talked too much in History of Fluxing.

She didn't talk *enough* in science, and got scolded for "low participation."

Mitali had told her they'd be playing kittenball during gym, and Nory had looked forward to it all day. But now that gym class was finally happening, she wasn't playing her best. Her kitten didn't have nice whiskers, her tail-whacking aim was terrible, and the yarn kept getting caught in her claws.

"You're still getting used to everything," Mitali said during a five-minute water break.

"You think?" Nory said. She felt nervous and tired.

"Show Coach Giovanni your dritten!" Mitali suggested. "That's your secret weapon!"

"Would she *want* me to turn into something wonky?"

Mitali stood. "Coach G! Coach G! Do you want to see Nory's dritten? It's her secret weapon on the kittenball court!"

"Her what?" said Coach G. She was burly and

wore a whistle around her neck. She had once played professional tigerball for the Palm City Rogues and she took sports very, very seriously.

"My dritten," Nory said hopefully. "Dragon-kitten? It's a kitten with a little bit of dragon. My coach at home checked the rule book. And it's totally okay. Do you want to see it? I don't mind. I can do it!"

The gym teacher tilted her head, which meant she was at least considering it, and Nory's body started to tingle. Just thinking about fluxing into a dritten cheered her up. She wanted to fly! And breathe fire! Breathe fire and meow at the same time!

"Please?" said Mitali. "It's really cool."

Nory held her breath.

"No," the teacher said. "Better not. I'd prefer everyone play as a kitten."

Nory's shoulders slumped.

Coach G blew her whistle. Slowly, Nory followed the others back onto the court.

She fluxed into Kitten-Nory. She stayed Kitten-Nory. With unimpressive whiskers.

She didn't score any goals.

She messed up her yaggle.

Her tail whacks went crooked.

She wished she were back at Dunwiddle.

The Sage Academy library had stained-glass windows and bookshelves so high that two librarians were flying as they reshelved the books.

Nory was here to find Pepper. They had arranged to meet after class.

"What's wrong?" Pepper asked, when Nory found her staring up at a huge, circular, stained-glass window.

"I need a lemon drop," Nory said.

"Poor Nory," Pepper said. "But guess what? Not only do I have lemon drops, I have the perfect place to eat them."

"You do?"

"Hush," Pepper said, and she pulled Nory to a door at the end of a long hall. She looked around to make sure no one was watching, then opened the door.

A supply closet!

It held two vacuum cleaners, many rolls of paper towels, spray cleaner, and a lot of other boring things, just like every supply closet everywhere. And yet! It was three times the size of the supply closet at Dunwiddle that had become Pepper and Nory's favorite hideout.

"I'm always on the lookout for a good hiding place," Pepper continued. "You never know when you'll need one."

With the door shut against the rest of the world, Pepper pulled a box of lemon drops from her pocket.

"This will be our new headquarters," Nory said. Then her eyes filled with tears. "Well, until Friday. But in January, I'll be here alone! Pepper! What will I do then?"

Pepper put her arm around Nory. "You'll rock Sage Academy just like you rocked UDM—that's what you'll do."

Nory went weepy. "Oh, Pepper, you're the best Pepper in the whole world," she said, resting her head on her friend's shoulder. "Who will give me lemon drops when you're gone? Who will hide in the closet with me? How will I ever survive at this strict school? I hate it here, Pepper, I hate it!" Tears streamed down her cheeks. "I can't look on the bright side anymore," Nory said. "There is no bright side!"

Pepper hugged her more tightly. Nory cried and cried.

"When life gives you lemons . . ." Pepper said when Nory was all cried out.

"I don't think I can make lemonade," Nory said. "Not today. Not here."

Pepper reached into her box of lemon drops and handed Nory one. "I was going to say, you take a lemon drop from your best friend."

10

During Tuesday's last class period, while Nory was at gym *not* turning into a dritten, the Flare students were at music.

Elliott's jaw dropped when he first saw the music room. *Wow!* It was fully soundproofed. There were eight pianos, lined up in two rows of four. A large collection of drums stood at the back of the room, next to twenty guitars.

There was even a birdcage in the corner, filled with fat yellow canaries. Elliott didn't understand what canaries would do in music class, but hey, canaries were cool.

The teacher, Ms. Terraform, asked the Sage kids to please take their seats at the pianos. Two kids per piano, with one kid next to the teacher. The Dunwiddle students sat in folding chairs.

Ms. Terraform lifted the birdcage and set it on a table. "I thought the Dunwiddle students might like to see what we're working on," she said. The six canaries arranged themselves on a long perch in a neat row.

The Sage students began to play. Each pair of students played the same duet. All of the students were in time with the others.

Then, after several minutes of impressive unison, the Sage kids let loose. Some kids added harmonies. Others added jazzy riffs. Then the canaries joined in! The Sage kids played, the canaries sang, and the room rang with joyful music.

When they finished, everyone burst into applause, with Elliott clapping the loudest. They were so good!

"We have to practice an hour a day, six days a week," said GJ, shrugging modestly when Elliott complimented him. "I could hardly play at all when I started."

During the next part of class, Ms. Terraform divided the kids into five bands, which they'd be in for the rest of the week. Within each band, she assigned at least one kid to be a keyboard player, one to be a guitar player, one to play the bass, one to be a drummer, and one to be a vocalist. Each band got a canary.

Elliott was grouped with all Sage kids, including GJ, who was learning bass. He'd been assigned guitar, which he'd been playing since he was four. His dad taught guitar lessons, after all.

"Today, just muddle through with your group as best you can," said Ms. Terraform to the Dunwiddle students. "If you do your homework, we'll get it sounding great by the end of Thursday's class, I promise."

A few minutes in, GJ raised his hand. "Elliott is really good," he told the teacher. "He's, like, a guitar expert."

Ms. Terraform raised her eyebrows. Elliott blushed, but continued playing.

"You have real skill," she said when he finished. "Why don't you come meet my sixth-grade rock band? The guitarist broke her thumb yesterday, poor girl. I bet they could use your help."

"Sure," said Elliott, glowing.

So, after class, Elliott stood in as guitar player with the sixth-grade rock band. The other members of the band were mostly Fuzzies, and they'd recruited a tambourine-shaking meerkat and a flamingo that played the triangle.

It was amazingly fun.

When practice ended, Elliott met up with Nory for afternoon tea in the Rose Parlor.

The Rose Parlor was painted pink. It had floral-print sofas and chairs, plus little tables that looked like they belonged to someone's great-grandmother. Mitali had explained that every Tuesday at four thirty, tea and cookies were served. Really good cookies.

Large plates of them. Chocolate cream filled, jam filled, chocolate chip, snickerdoodles.

Nory and Elliott put their cookies on pink china plates. Ms. Fujita served them tea in fragile cups with saucers. There were hardly any fifth graders there. It was mostly older students who crossed their legs and only took two or three cookies.

Nory found a spot to sit and squeezed Elliott's forearm so hard it hurt. "Elliott," she said urgently. "You're my best friend. You and Pepper. You know that, right?"

"Yeah, sure," Elliott said. He wondered what she was getting at.

"Will you promise to call me every day when I go to Sage full-time?"

"I guess so," said Elliott, who didn't love talking on the phone.

"Even if you can't, *promise* me we'll stay friends, always and forever."

"I promise. Here, eat this," he said. "The snicker-doodles are really good."

"Not important!" Nory cried. "Elliott, how will you live without me in Dunwiddle? You'll be so lonely!"

Elliott thought. He *would* miss Nory, absolutely. But unlike Nory, he'd have Willa and Andres and the rest of the UDM kids. He'd be okay.

Nory started to cry. "You'll have no one to walk to school with. You'll have no one to play with. My desk next to you will be empty and you'll just stare at it, wondering how I'm doing, and not even listening to the teacher!"

She sobbed onto his shoulder. Elliott patted her uncertainly.

"You're going to flunk the second half of fifth grade because you'll miss me so much!" Nory wailed. "I'm really worried about you!"

Elliott snagged another snickerdoodle from the nearest tray. He broke it in two and gave half to Nory. "Snickerdoodle promise," he told her. "We'll always be friends, and I'll focus really hard on not flunking out. Okay?"

A fat tear rolled down Nory's cheek. She took a sip of her tea and made a face.

Elliott finished his snickerdoodle and helped himself to a butter cookie filled with apricot jam. He looked at the Sage Fuzzies, who were giving their rabbit companions bites of brown sugar biscuits. He watched a Flare heat up the milk for her tea, foaming it like an espresso machine. He looked at the red velvet curtains and the lovely way they framed the view of the garden.

Maybe Sage wasn't the right school for Nory. But for the kids it was right for?

Those kids were the luckiest kids he'd ever known.

11

Tuesday night, everyone met for a Sage Academy end-of-term tradition, the annual hide-and-seek.

After dinner at home with her family, Nory headed straight to the Hall of Magic and Performance and snagged a seat next to Mitali. The other UDM kids were a couple of rows ahead.

Father strode to the center of the stage. "Most of you know this already, but for our fifth graders and our guests from Dunwiddle Magic School: Tonight is a chance for the senior Flickers and the Flicker faculty to test your wits!"

A cheer went up. The younger Flickers began to chant: "Flick-ers! Flick-ers!"

"Ahem." Father coughed.

The young Flickers went silent.

"The hide-and-seek shall take place in the main building. First, the Flickers will be dismissed and given five minutes to hide. All three floors are fair game. Then, when so directed, the rest of you will seek them."

Mitali leaned over to Nory. "I've heard it's super fun. Did you go to the hide-and-seek when you were little?"

Nory shook her head. She'd always been *too* little, according to Father.

Father was telling everyone the rules. "You must not use paint. Or powdered sugar. Or anything else messy that might help you locate a hiding Flicker if you tossed it in the right direction. Flyers, you may not assist your Flicker friends by flying them out of reach. You are not licensed to take passengers, and I don't want to see a repeat of last year's chimney hijinks. The only Flicker who can fly in this game is our double talent, Kinnette."

"There are a lot of rules," Nory whispered to Mitali. "How are we supposed to have fun with so many rules?"

Mitali shrugged. "All our games have lots of rules."

"Fluxers *may* flux into creatures with night vision or powerful senses of smell," said Father. "Fuzzies, however, may not enlist the aid of animal companions. Those animals are not students here, and this game is only for students of Sage Academy!"

"And Dunwiddle!" called out Rune.

Father gave him a look. "I stand corrected." He continued. "Flares may not heat, smoke, or use fire in any way to expose a Flicker's location. Each found Flicker is one point. Reminder that Flickers must become visible immediately upon being found and will report back here to Ms. Fujita. We have thirty senior Flickers, eight Flicker faculty members, one staff member, and me, for a total of forty Flickers fighting fortune's finding."

He looked hopefully at the audience, perhaps expecting awe at his use of alliteration. When he received no reaction, he cleared his throat. "The game ends at ten p.m. If, at that time, three or more Flickers remain undiscovered, the Flicker students will all be treated to a movie night on Friday. What's more, the student who has the most points wins a new laptop."

The Flickers gave an enormous cheer.

"I hear no one ever finds your father," said Mitali. "Not ever. Do you by any chance know his secret hiding place?"

Nory did not.

"All right," announced Father. "Use your ears. Your noses. Your well-educated intelligence. And good luck."

With that, he and all the senior Flickers disappeared. Nory could hear them getting out of their seats, saying "Good luck, suckers!" to their non-Flicker friends as they hurried out of the hall.

Ms. Fujita set a timer for five minutes. "You may speak among yourselves and strategize until the hide-and-seek begins!"

"We could try puppy," Nory said to Mitali. "As puppies, we'd have a good sense of smell. But my puppy goes upside down pretty easily."

"*All* the fifth-grade Fluxers will be doing puppy," said Mitali. "And the older Fluxers can do tracking breeds like bloodhounds. There's no point in doing that. I was thinking I might try my robin? I could fly around and maybe find Kinnette."

"Won't the Flyers be up looking for her?"

"But they won't be tiny. I could slip into nooks and crannies. They can't."

Nory wasn't sure that would actually help. And she was still wondering what *she* could do to find the Flickers when the timer went off. The hunt was on!

Pepper and Marigold ran up to Nory, full of excitement. "If I fierce the fluxed students, that could clear the way for one of you to win the laptop," said Pepper, grabbing Nory's arm.

Oohh! *That* was a great idea!

They jogged across the lawn to the main building, going inside just as Sebastian tagged a Flicker boy who was hiding behind a coat of arms in the hallway. The boy flickered back to visible. "Aw, man!" he complained. Then, with a sigh, he asked, "Whom shall I say hath found me?" Apparently, that was the traditional Flicker thing to say when caught.

"Sebastian Boondoggle," said Sebastian.

The boy slouched off.

Of *course*. Sebastian could see invisible things! And that included invisible people!

Sebastian opened the door to an apparently empty classroom, walked across to the teacher's desk, and tagged the Flicker hiding under it. The girl stomped her feet as she came into view. "Ugh! So annoying. Whom shall I say hath found me?"

"Sebastian Boondoggle." Nory and her friends trailed Sebastian as he walked easily through the building, gently tagging Flicker after Flicker. Wherever they went, students fluxed into bloodhounds and beagles ran away because of Pepper's fiercing, or popped back into human form.

In one classroom, Pepper scared a Fluxer pig that must have weighed eight hundred pounds. In the college guidance office, a large brown bear dropped to its belly and crawled into a corner in fear. Then Pepper paused her magic for a minute. The bear fluxed into a very cranky senior girl. "I'm not sure using upside-down magic is fair," she said.

"Dr. Horace listed all the rules," said Mitali. "He didn't say not to."

"Well, there's a Flicker in here wearing way too much perfume," said the girl as she stormed off. "Good luck finding her without me sniffing her out."

It was Kinnette. Sebastian saw her easily, floating on the ceiling. He asked Andres for help tagging her. Andres took off his brickpack and tapped her quickly on the shoulder.

"Whom shall I say hath found me?" Kinnette asked.

"You take this one, Andres," said Sebastian.

"Andres Padillo," cheered Andres.

Sebastian found all forty of the invisible Flickers within ten minutes. Ten minutes! It was a new Sage record, Mitali told Nory gleefully.

Father was the last to be found, but he was found nonetheless—for the first time in Sage history. He was sitting, cross-legged but still dignified, on top of his own set of filing cabinets.

Nory could tell that Father was not pleased. He got down from the cabinet by stepping on a small table. Nory knew he wouldn't like doing such an awkward thing in front of the students.

"Whom shall I say hath found me?" he asked Sebastian.

"It's my friend Sebastian," Nory blurted, wanting Father to be kind to her friends. "Aren't his powers amazing?"

"Quite," said Father sourly.

Once Father reported himself found, a gong sounded. Everyone hurried out of the main building and across the lawn to the Hall of Magic and Performance.

Father announced that Sebastian Boondoggle from Dunwiddle had won the laptop. The Flickers grumbled and mumbled, and Nory bit her lower lip. She was happy for Sebastian, but now the Flickers wouldn't get their movie night, ending a ten-year streak of winning.

And the rest of the kids hadn't gotten to enjoy the big hunt.

"Well, that sure was fun," she heard one of the sixth-grade Fluxers grouse. "Not!"

"We barely got to do any seeking!" said someone else.

Both complainers *glared* at Sebastian.

Unlike her friend, Nory wasn't an Upside-Down Flicker. She couldn't see the bolts of anger she was sure the non-UDM kids were shooting at them, but she sure could feel them.

12

"Okay, students," Dr. Vogel announced, Wednesday in Flare class. "Fill your jars with cold tap water. We'll be heating the water to ninety degrees precisely, and I want you to aim for speed and accuracy."

Everyone filled their jars and took out their thermometers.

Elliott was worried. He could *not* heat his water in less than seventy seconds. He just couldn't do it. He'd keep trying, but he wasn't sure it would ever work.

Dr. Vogel went around the room checking people's times.

She stood in front of Lacey. "You were able to do it in under ten seconds, correct?"

"Um, yup," Lacey said.

"Excuse me?" Dr. Vogel said.

Lacey's cheeks turned pink. "Yes I was, Dr. Vogel."

"Let's see."

Lacey placed her thermometer in the glass and then her hands on the jar. She focused on the jar, her jaw clenched in determination.

"Go," the teacher said, pressing the timer.

At ten seconds, the thermometer said sixty-five degrees. At twenty seconds, it was at seventy-nine. At thirty it was at only eighty-eight. Lacey finally hit ninety degrees at thirty-nine seconds.

The teacher's eyebrows were raised.

"There's something wrong with this thermometer," Lacey protested. "I did it in under ten back in the dorms."

"Mmm," said the teacher.

"Or maybe my water started off colder than everyone else's." Lacey glared at Elliott. "I bet the wonko froze it. You did, didn't you?"

"No, Lacey, I didn't," he said.

Dr. Vogel turned to Elliott. "You're up."

Elliott took a deep breath and picked up his jar. "I don't think I can beat seventy-two seconds," he told her. "That's the best I did in my homework."

Dr. Vogel nodded. Elliott began. He focused all his energy on the water in his jar, trying to push heat out of his body and into the water.

Lacey and Rune tittered.

"I just grew a beard waiting," Rune said.

"He's the worst at Dunwiddle, too," Lacey explained to the Sage student next to her. "He's in the special slow class and everything."

Elliott tried to ignore them.

Hotter. Hotter. Hotter. The water heated up to the required temperature in sixty-seven seconds!

"Better than you led me to expect," Dr. Vogel said. "A question: Do your hands get cold halfway through?"

Elliott was surprised. How did she know? "Um, yeah," he said apologetically. "I have to fight off the cold."

"Have you ever tried Hex gloves?"

"What are those?"

"They're special gloves that just came out a few years ago. They're supposed to help Flares with pinched nerves." Dr. Vogel tapped her chin. "I wonder if your freezing magic is pinching your flaring magic. Want to try the gloves? I have a pair in my desk."

She rummaged through her drawer and returned with a pair of black fingerless gloves. They were leather, and tight on his wrists.

She brought Elliott a jar of fresh tap water.

He tried again to heat the water, and this time when he pushed on his magic, his hands stayed hot! The freezing didn't overtake his flaring!

"Twenty-three seconds," said Dr. Vogel, checking her stopwatch. "Very nice."

"Whoa!" Elliott said.

The teacher smiled. "Hold on to the Hex gloves while you're here. I think they'll help you."

Elliott flexed his hands and admired the gloves. "Thanks!"

"I'll need them back before you return to Dunwiddle. They're expensive, unfortunately," said Dr. Vogel.

She went on to the next student. As soon as she was out of hearing distance, Lacey glared at Elliott and said, "They don't accept half robots at Sage."

"I never applied to Sage," Elliott said. "I'm here as a visitor, just like you."

"I'm first on the wait list, you know."

"I know, Lacey. We all know."

GJ caught Elliott's eye and stuck his finger in his mouth, pretending to barf. Elliott grinned.

• • •

Mitali was in Elliott's Science of Fire class, which came next. Since she was a double talent, she had homeroom with the Fluxers, but took some classes with the Flares.

"Elliott!" she called out. "Sit by me. Be my partner."

They followed the instructions on the board, heating a red liquid over a Bunsen burner and stirring in two tablespoons of green powder.

The liquid fizzed.

"Why is ours fizzing?" Mitali whispered. She glanced around the room. "No one else's is fizzing."

Now the liquid was, like, *burping*. Big bubbles formed, shimmered, and popped.

Elliott reread the lab instructions.

Uh-oh. They'd missed a step.

"We were supposed to squeeze in three drops of purple gel *before* adding the green powder," he said.

A huge fireball rose violently from their jar.

"Oh, no!" Mitali cried, rearing back from the heat.

The fireball turned pink and rolled across the

ceiling, burning the paint and leaving a trail of cracks and blisters.

Elliott lifted his hands to freeze the ball. *Zwoop!*

Instead of ice, a burst of flame shot out from his fingertips. It was because of the Hex gloves, which he hadn't taken off!

He ripped the gloves off and iced the pink fireball. It froze into a bubble and hung from the ceiling.

"Quick thinking!" Mitali said. "No one even had to use the fire extinguisher—and we have to use them *all the time* in this class. Look at you, saving ceilings one class period at a time!"

"Ha," said Elliott, pleased. "Thanks."

Mitali touched one of the gloves on his desk. "Are those Hex gloves?"

"Yeah. They help my flaring. But they stop my ice, I think."

"But you *can* flare? If you're wearing the gloves?"

"Much better than I can without."

"Lemme see."

Elliott tugged one of the gloves onto his right

hand. He focused on flaring, and a little flame burst from his right index finger.

"Can you freeze with the other hand?" Mitali asked.

Elliott raised his left hand and pushed on his freezing magic. A small icicle formed, extending from his left index finger like a really long, clear nail.

Mitali jumped up and down. "Can you do both at the same time?"

"I don't know," Elliott said. He thought for a moment. If he kept the Hex glove on his right hand and left his other hand bare, then . . . maybe? He pointed both index fingers. He took a deep breath. He focused on his magic, and *sleesh-sizzle-pop*! A stream of ice *and* fire collided overhead!

"Dude," said Mitali. "If freezing was its own type of magic, you'd be a double talent."

He smiled. "My friend Marigold thinks the ice *is* its own type of magic. She says I'm a Freezer."

"A Freezer *and* a Flare," Mitali said excitedly. "Hey, listen. I'm part of the double-talent affinity group, and we're meeting this afternoon. Do you want to come?"

"Really?" Elliott asked. "Me?"

"Yes, you!" she said. "It'll be fun."

13

There he is," Nory heard someone say at lunch. "That's the Boondoggle kid."

Sebastian was sitting next to her, eating a serving of apple cobbler bigged-up by Marigold.

Nory looked over her shoulder and saw two boys. Miller was the redheaded guy Sebastian had seen peeing in the pool. The other boy was reed thin and had a neck that was not much larger than his tie.

Something whizzed past Nory and bounced off Sebastian's skull. His head bobbled with the impact, but he didn't do anything.

Ugh. What did they even throw? Nory searched the floor beneath Sebastian's seat and found a wad of bread. A *wet* wad of bread.

"Those boys threw a spit-bread-ball at you!" she whispered.

Sebastian shook his head disdainfully, then went back to eating.

Nory picked up the spit-bread-ball, trying to make as little skin-to-bread contact as possible. She went to Miller's table. "Excuse me, but I believe this is yours." She plopped it onto his plate.

"Tell your Flicker friend he ruined hide-and-seek last night," said the boy with the skinny neck. "He's a waste of space and should make *himself* invisible. Except—oh, wait. He can't, can he? Too wonky."

"And whom shall I say is sending this message?" Nory asked in a steely voice.

Suddenly, Miller's table monitor was standing over them. He was frighteningly tall and intense. "Hello," he said. "I am Monitor Hoggins. At Sage, students remain seated throughout the meal." He beckoned to Monitor Sorbee, who rose and came over. "If you can't control your table," he said to her, "I'll tell the head of lunch patrol."

"They started it," Nory protested. "They threw a spit-bread-ball at my friend."

Miller pointed at Sebastian. "Because he's the kid who ruined hide-and-seek."

Monitor Hoggins pressed his lips together. "Is that so?"

Sorbee crossed her arms over her chest. "Uncool," she said. "Spit-bread-balls are the least of what he deserves."

Sebastian put down his fork and said, "The game was hide-and-seek. You guys hid. I found you."

"You ruined the game for all of us," Miller said.

Pink spots rose on Sebastian's cheeks.

Nory wanted to stand up for her friend. She wanted to flux into a dritten and roar at these mean kids with her fire breath. Sebastian had won fair and square! The Sage kids were being sore losers!

"Nory, let it go," Sebastian said. "If our table loses points, Sorbee's going to blame you."

With a jolt, Nory realized that Sebastian was looking out for *her*.

It was Nory who needed to make friends here. Sebastian would return to Dunwiddle at the end of the week and never see any of these people again.

She ducked her head and returned to her seat.

In writing class, Nory got in trouble for her penmanship. Her *Q*'s, it seemed, were too swirly.

In fluxing class, she got in trouble for adding squid legs to her puppy, even though she sat and stood and lay down exactly when she was supposed to.

By the time she got home, all Nory wanted to do was curl up with Dalia's rabbits. Or take a nice hot bath with so many bubbles that she could disappear into them.

But she had homework to do: loads and loads of boring boringness.

She dropped into her chair at the kitchen table, where Dalia and Hawthorn were already hard at work on their own homework.

"So many assignments," Nory moaned. "I have something in every single class!"

Dalia gave her a funny smile, then went back to scribbling notes. She was adding lots of exclamation points and smilies. Smilies!

Hawthorn said, "Nory, shh. I'm reading about architecture and how buildings affect the way we live. It's fascinating."

Nory stared at her brother and sister. She loved them, but she felt so different from them.

They were sitting right there, but she felt alone.

At dinner, Nory pushed her food around on her plate. How could she eat when her stomach was all tight and achy?

"Nory, is there a problem?" Father asked.

She blinked.

Father had noticed! He'd actually noticed how she was doing, and he actually seemed to care!

Before she lost her nerve, she said, "Yes! It's me! I'm the problem!"

Father tilted his head.

"I mean Sage! I mean, me at Sage. That's the problem. Can I please please please go back to Dunwiddle?" Nory pleaded. "When the buildings are repaired, I mean. I'd be much happier there."

Father looked baffled. "What in the world are you talking about?"

"Um. I fit better there, I think. At Dunwiddle." Nory stole a glance at Hawthorn. "Because of the architecture and stuff?"

"Don't be silly," said Father. "You love Sage."

"Actually, I don't," Nory said.

Instead of responding, Father started talking to Dalia about the skunk test she'd taken the day before, an important part of Fuzzy finals for eighth graders. She had gotten the highest grade in her class.

Either Father hadn't heard Nory, or he had pretended not to.

• • •

Later, Hawthorn rapped on Nory's bedroom door. "I wanted to check on you," he said, entering and sitting at the foot of her bed. "Because at dinner—" He broke off. "Nory? Are you crying?"

Nory put her face in her pillow. She hiccuped.

"It's hard adjusting to a new place," Hawthorn said awkwardly. "But everyone struggles at first, in new situations."

Nory cried harder. She always cried harder when she was sad and people were nice to her. "I h-h-hate it so much," she managed to say.

Dalia appeared in the doorway. "Nory? Hawthorn?"

"Nory's sad," Hawthorn said. "She knows she'll settle into Sage just fine"—he glanced at Nory and nodded encouragingly—"but right now, it's challenging."

Nory knew she would never settle into Sage. Never.

"Oh, Nory," Dalia said, joining them on Nory's

bed. "We're so glad you're here. We missed you so much when you were with Aunt Margo. All of us, Father included."

"You are a Horace," Hawthorn said. "Sage is where you belong. You're having growing pains, that's all. You've got this, Nory."

"But . . ." Nory said. But what? Hawthorn's eyes were kind, and he wanted to cheer her up, but he wasn't really listening, either.

"I have an idea," Dalia said. "Tomorrow morning, we'll go to campus early, just you and me. Okay, Nory?"

"Why?" Nory said, sniffing.

"Because!" Dalia said. She beamed. "I know just how to cheer you up. I can't believe I didn't think of it until now!"

"What is it?"

"Nope, not going to tell." Dalia squeezed Nory in a sideways hug. "But you will love it. And you'll see that Sage isn't all that bad, I promise."

14

The double-talent affinity group met on Wednesday, after classes were over for the day. Elliott followed Mitali up a long, winding staircase to the very top of a tower. Through a heavy wooden door was a circular room, with stone walls. Elliott felt like he was in a fairy tale.

Kinnette was there already. She was the senior Flicker-Flyer Nory's dad had mentioned during hide-and-seek. She was lean and wore a headscarf, and her arms were invisible, though her hands were not.

"Sorry not to be entirely present, ha-ha," said Kinnette to Elliott in a friendly way. One of her hands rose through the air, and Elliott shook it. "I have an invisibility exam tomorrow, so I'm practicing. They grade us by the inch."

The other members of the group arrived—two kids, two sloths, and one kangaroo—and introductions were made all around. In addition to Mitali and Kinnette, the double-talent group consisted of a seventh-grade girl named Dawn, who was a Flyer-Fuzzy; a ninth-grade girl named Prairie, who was a Flyer-Flare; and an eleventh-grade boy named David, who was a Fuzzy-Fluxer. He was in the shape of a tree sloth, and he was accompanied by an actual sloth. The two sloths looked identical as far as Elliott could tell, but apparently all the others could tell them apart.

The kangaroo turned out to be Ms. Cheddarlegs, who taught magic history and regular history. She served as the faculty leader for the group.

"Excuse the kangaroo," she said to Elliott after fluxing into her human form. "And please don't tell Dr. Horace. But it's much easier to get up the stairs in marsupial form than in the form of a fifty-year-old human with chronic knee problems."

Ms. Cheddarlegs wore sheer pantyhose, and initially, Elliott felt wary of her. Then she passed out red licorice, which just went to prove that first impressions really shouldn't be trusted. Everyone sat around a big table in the center of the room, except for the sloths, who climbed onto a coatrack and settled themselves there.

It wasn't a touchy-feely talk session, the way it would have been if Ms. Starr had been running it. Nobody revealed their emotions or shared things about their day. Instead, the meeting was divided into two parts.

First, Ms. Cheddarlegs shared news articles about double talents. One was about issues specific to double-talent education. "As double talents, we have to be mindful about mixing our magic," she said. "For some of us, our two talents should never be used together. Mixing them might tangle up the magic. I do not flare while fluxed, and neither does Mitali. But in other talent mixes, there's more lee-way. David, obviously, is using his Fluxer magic. He's a sloth! And at the same time, he's using his Fuzzy magic."

One of the sloths jumped down from the coatrack and popped into boy shape. Boy-David was slightly stooped and wore thick glasses. "I was taught that it's very important never to lose track of my human mind," he said. "But if I want to be the strongest Fuzzy I can be, I actually need to let go of my human mind a bit and get in touch with the sloth mind. I've discovered that if I follow the rules, then when I'm in animal form I can't communicate with animals very well. My fuzzying is low-level. In order to truly befriend my sloth, I have to break the rules and let my human mind go."

"Interesting," said Ms. Cheddarlegs. "Some edu-cators, including those who have been studying upside-down magic, think that certain rules might indeed be limiting our magic abilities."

At the mention of upside-down magic, Elliott sat up straighter.

The second half of the meeting was more like coaching. The students made short presentations about their double talents. Dawn told them that her flying was going really well, but in Fuzzy classes she was struggling whenever she had to interact with more than one animal.

People made suggestions: David said that sometimes it was easier to get along with groups of a certain species. "We all do mice in seventh grade, but maybe you're better with groups of insects, or schools of fish, or something," he said.

"Sometimes double talents have unique abilities in one area," confirmed Ms. Cheddarlegs. "I never was much good at kittens and puppies, and I worried that—" Here, she looked at Elliott and paused. "I worried I was never going to be able to do more difficult animals," she said finally. "But marsupial fluxing turned out to be very natural to me—and my kitten still isn't that good!" She laughed.

After the others had presented, Mitali stood up. She looked nervous.

"If Ms. Cheddarlegs hadn't talked about the different educational ideas about double talents, and if Elliott wasn't here, I don't think I'd be showing you guys this," she confessed.

Elliott leaned forward.

Mitali took a breath. She lifted her chin. Then she fluxed into a small brown bird with an orangey-red throat and belly. A robin!

Robin-Mitali flew around the room. The other students clapped.

Then Robin-Mitali breathed fire. A big burst of fire, directed at the stone wall.

Everyone fell silent.

Robin-Mitali landed on the floor and fluxed back to a girl. "I know Fluxer-Flares aren't supposed to mix our magics," she said. "But it just feels natural to me. Please don't tell my teachers," she added. "I don't want them to know."

Ms. Cheddarlegs fluxed into kangaroo and hopped over to Mitali. She thumped her tail consolingly and patted Mitali's shoulder.

"We won't tell," said Dawn, Kinnette, and the others.

At the end of the meeting, Mitali asked Elliott to show his freezing magic. Kangaroo-Cheddarlegs turned back into a teacher and sparked a fire in the hearth with a flip of her wrist. Elliott iced the logs, putting out the fire and spreading frost across the stone and out across the wall.

"It's beautiful!" cried Mitali.

"I've never seen anything like it," said the teacher.

"My control is getting better," said Elliott. "I think Dr. Vogel's fire-breathing exercises are making my magic stronger. But I still ice things by accident sometimes, and I really need to use a Hex glove if I want my flaring to work. Which I'd never even tried until today. So I don't know if I'm actually a double talent."

"Honestly, I don't know either," said the teacher. "But as long as you're here at Sage, you're welcome to attend our affinity group."

"I'll be gone on Friday," said Elliott, feeling sad. "As long as the repairs to my real school get done on time."

"Ah," said Ms. Cheddarlegs. "Well, we will miss you."

Elliott gave her a wobbly smile. He would miss them, too.

15

Nory's feet dragged as she put on her uniform Thursday morning.

Thick tights, ugh.

Pleated skirt, ugh.

Tie and blazer, double ugh.

She felt annoyed at her old room in Father's house. It was painted pale pink and had a white nightstand that matched her white dresser. All things that had been chosen when she was a baby. Her room at Aunt Margo's was much more of a middle schooler room.

She cheered up, though, when she remembered she was leaving the house early with Dalia. She ate her hard-boiled egg and grabbed an apple to munch on while they walked to Sage. The day smelled like snow, but it wasn't snowing. It was the kind of crisp winter weather where the wind bites your face.

Dalia took Nory past the Fuzzy building to the back entrance to the Hall of Magic and Performance. There, surrounded by a low stone wall, stood a greenhouse. Its windows were steamed up and Nory could see plants inside. Dalia led Nory to where they could peek in.

The ground inside the greenhouse was covered with moss, though there was also a path you could walk on. There were pots of flowers, bushes and trees, plus a number of hollow logs and what looked like hutches made of wood.

Puttering about, going in and out of hutches, sniffing all around the place, were about thirty skunks. They had fluffy patches of white on their heads and two stripes down their backs. All of them were bright-eyed and bushy-tailed.

"They're so cute!" said Nory.

"Aren't they?" said Dalia. "Some Fuzzies don't like them, but I think I might like them even more than rabbits. They get up to more mischief. I like to come here when I'm feeling sad, or when I need to think. My Fuzzy teacher showed me where the key is. She only shows it to the students she likes best."

Dalia bent to the low stone wall that surrounded the greenhouse. She pressed her palm against one particular stone and used her finger to dislodge a large, ornate stone key that had been fitted there, almost invisibly. "Don't tell where the secret key is, 'kay?"

Nory promised she wouldn't.

A wave of warm air hit Nory as they entered the skunk garden. She took off her winter coat and scarf and hung them on a hook. "Won't we get sprayed?" she asked as they walked farther in.

"No, I know what I'm doing," said Dalia proudly. "I aced my skunk exam, remember?"

As Dalia's Fuzzy magic began to work, the skunks toddled out of their habitats and came to meet Nory. Nory sat down on a hollow log and stretched her fingers out to let them be sniffed.

One of them wiggled its bottom and then jumped, catlike, onto her lap.

"Without Fuzzy magic, you could never pet them," said Dalia. "They're not friendly to humans."

Nory knew Fuzzies could befriend all sorts of animals, even wild animals, if they put in enough practice. But she'd never had the chance to meet any wild animals herself, except the dragons during her Dragon Haven field trip.

A second skunk jumped onto her lap. "Those two are best friends," said Dalia. "Their names are Domino and Penguin."

Dalia gave Nory a handful of raisins from her pocket. "You can feed them if you want. They love fruit."

"Even pineapple?" Nory disliked pineapple. She fed the raisins to Domino and Penguin, who nibbled them gently from her palm.

"Even pineapple," said Dalia. "Cranberries make them go wild, though."

"Wild? What do you mean?"

"Cranberries are like catnip for them. I brought one cranberry so you can see," said Dalia. She pulled it out of her pocket. Immediately, Domino and Penguin leapt off Nory's lap and ran to Dalia, sitting on their hind legs in a begging position. All the others followed, until Dalia was encircled by thirty begging skunks.

She bent down and offered the cranberry to Penguin, who practically inhaled it. Then she held up her empty hands. "That's all, sorry!" she told the skunks. "No way am I letting you all go wild. Not on my watch!"

When Nory saw how Penguin acted after gobbling the cranberry, she understood Dalia's caution. First, he ran around in circles. Then he bounded high in the air, as if jumping on a trampoline, several times. Then he ran up and down the small indoor trees like a cat in a frenzy, finally stopping for breath high on a branch.

Gently, Dalia lifted him off the branch and set him down. "He goes up there and then he's stuck," she explained. "Cranberries! What can I say?" Now on the mossy floor, Penguin rolled back and forth, waving his front paws.

Nory stroked Penguin's belly. "I've fluxed into skunk before," she told Dalia, "but never without adding some other animal. I mostly add elephant, actually."

"That must be dramatic."

"Oh yeah." Nory told Dalia the whole story of her disastrous first day at Dunwiddle, when Lacey Clench had upset her so much she'd fluxed into an enormous skunkephant and skunk-sprayed half the people in the school cafeteria.

Dalia laughed. Not a mean laugh. Not *at* Nory. Just at the idea of a skunkephant in a school cafeteria.

Nory laughed, too. It hadn't been funny at the time, but now that she'd made friends and was happy at Dunwiddle, it was easy to see the humor.

"How come you want to go back to Dunwiddle?" asked Dalia. "I know there's no skunk garden there. And there's definitely no special pool for fish fluxing lessons, or a monkey gym for primate fluxing class. Plus you told me yourself the cafeteria food was gross."

Nory petted the skunks. "I feel like myself at Dunwiddle," she said. "And like I'm learning to be my *best* self. I can't say I won't like the monkey gym here at Sage, but I want to wear my own clothes. And have a teacher who really likes me. And a principal who listens to my ideas, at least some of the time. I have a kittenball coach who thinks my dritten will be great on the field, and I have friends who understand what it's like to be UDM."

"Well, it's true you won't get any of that at Sage," said Dalia. "But you *will* get me! And I know you'll be all right." She stood and offered her hand to Nory. Nory took it and stood up.

"Thanks for taking me here," said Nory.

"I'll bring you back anytime," said Dalia. "Just let me know."

16

The skunk garden had been glorious. The *skunks* had been glorious.

But the rest of Thursday was stinky.

Mean looks? Check.

Boring silence? Check.

Do this, do this, do that? Check check check.

At lunch, Marigold bigged up everyone's corn bread and chocolate pudding, but Monitor Sorbee strode over with pursed lips when Pepper's pudding cup ended up the size of a cantaloupe.

"That is too much pudding," she scolded. "You'll vomit if you finish it. Also, Marigold, you're distracting your tablemates with upside-down magic during mealtime. I insist you leave the food alone."

"Yes, Monitor," said Marigold, who then winked at Pepper.

Nory looked around at her friends. How could they be talking and winking and eating pudding when Sorbee was mean and they all had ties on? They seemed unreasonably happy.

Suddenly, Lacey Clench dropped into the seat directly across from Nory—and Sorbee didn't even notice! How come Sorbee saw Pepper's giant pudding cup, but not Lacey being out of her seat? Ugh.

"Why do *you* look miserable?" Lacey asked.

"It's been a tough week."

"What? You've got it made. You're a Sage Academy student."

"Maybe I don't want to be here," Nory said, sighing. "Have you ever thought of that?"

Lacey snapped. "Are you that wonky that you don't even realize how lucky you are?"

"Not everyone wants what you want, Lacey." Nory looked at her friends for backup, but they were all involved in other conversations.

Lacey rolled her eyes. "If you're so unhappy, just wonk out and get expelled! Turn into your disgusting skunkephant and spray everyone. They will escort you right out of here, I promise you that. And then I'd get your spot. Which is rightfully mine, anyway."

Nory almost laughed out loud. Imagine if she turned into a skunkephant right here in the cafeteria! She'd spray stinky skunk smell on everyone. And on the food! She'd break, like, seven hundred rules, and make Monitor Sorbee super mad, and . . . oh!

I really could get kicked out! Nory realized. *They'd send me back to Dunwiddle!*

Yes, yes, yes! That's what she would do. That's what she would do RIGHT NOW, before she could chicken out!

"Okay," Nory said. "I'm going to do it."

Lacey's eyes gleamed. "What? Really? No! Really?"

"Yup, here goes!" Nory took a great inhale and thought of those dear sweet skunks in the skunk garden. Her bones cracked and popped. Her skin rippled. Then she invited elephant to mix with her skunk.

But something was wrong.

Lacey was growing bigger and bigger.

No, no. Lacey wasn't growing bigger. *Nory* was growing smaller . . . and smaller and smaller!

What was happening? Lacey's face loomed over her. Nory felt dizzy and strange.

"YOU KNOW YOU'RE SUPPOSED TO BE A SKUNKEPHANT!" Lacey yelled. "WHY ARE YOU JUST A SKUNK? AND WHY ARE YOU SO TINY?"

Tiny-Skunk-Nory was about the size of a teacup. There was no elephant in her, not one drop.

What happened next happened quickly.

Tiny-Skunk-Nory saw a giant face attached to a giant body.

It was Pepper. Pepper the Fierce, and her looming face was the scariest thing Tiny-Skunk-Nory had ever seen. She felt Pepper's fiercing magic zoom at her.

Run, run, run!

Tiny-Skunk-Nory ran, ran, ran.

Out of the cafeteria!

Out of the building!

Into the courtyard! And . . .

Plip!

Nory fluxed back into her girl-self.

She leaned over, pressing her hands to her legs and sucking in air.

She was alone.

Had anyone but Lacey and Pepper even seen her tiny skunk?

And why had she gone tiny? Marigold hadn't shrunk her.

She'd felt panicky. Itchy. Weak.

She hadn't been able to put elephant into her skunk, not one measly elephant toenail or elephant hair. And her skunk had been so strangely small!

Also, never mind what was going on with her magic, tiny skunk had not gotten her expelled. And her new goal was to get kicked out of Sage, so she could go back to Dunwiddle.

But maybe she could try again?

What could she do that would get her kicked out of Sage once and for all?

It was ten minutes until Thursday night's teeth-brushing time. Andres and Elliott were returning to their dorm together, after an optional evening study session. Andres was on his leash, and Elliot held the other end.

"I keep thinking about how tonight is our last night," Andres said. "I'm getting used to being here."

Elliott craned his neck and looked up at him. "It's bittersweet to think about leaving, huh?"

Andres nodded. "I miss my sister, though," he confessed. "Carmen always comes to talk to me before bedtime, and we play cards. I don't like sleeping in a dormitory. Or sleeping in my brickpack." At home, Andres's parents had created a bed for him on the ceiling. There was no such setup here.

"I can't blame you," said Elliott. "Sleeping in a brickpack: blech. But I think the dorm is pretty fun."

They walked along the path. Ahead and to the right was a topiary garden, the trees trimmed to look like math symbols. To the left was the canteen, where students could get hot chocolate with alphabet-shaped marshmallows. It was closed now. Above were stars and stars.

They reached the dorm, which was flooded in a gentle golden glow of light. Elliott heard voices from inside, kids laughing and goofing around. He paused outside the main door. He knew, when they went in, he would be caught up in the bustle of his friends in pajamas, his friends whacking each other with pillows, his friends brushing their teeth and spitting foam into the porcelain sinks. He was excited to step inside and be part of it all.

But he wanted to savor this "before" moment just a little longer, because being out here with Andres was really good, too.

"Will you miss Sage?" he asked Andres.

"I'll miss the Flyer teacher a little. And my Flyer friends." Andres bobbed in the wind. The leash tightened and pulled against Elliott's hand. "But mainly I'm ready to go home. You?"

"Yeah, sure," Elliott said automatically. "I mean, we get what we get, right?"

"What do you mean?" Andres asked.

"Oh, nothing," Elliott said, a little embarrassed. He pushed open the heavy dormitory door, and warm air enveloped him. Buxbom Dorm smelled like clean laundry and lemon-scented floor polish, plus a musty smell that grew stronger whenever the building's ancient heater kicked on.

Elliott would miss this smell.

He would miss Sage, period.

Was that what growing up and experiencing new things meant? No matter where he was, would there always be something to miss from wherever he wasn't? It didn't seem fair.

Andres whooped as he flew past Elliott into the dorm. He unhooked the lead from his leash and dropped it down. Elliott caught it.

Andres soared to the ceiling and did a flip turn. He pushed off the ceiling with his sneakers and extended his arms, dive-bombing Sebastian and Pepper, who shrieked.

"Tally-ho!" he crowed.

Elliott laughed. He ran after Andres, jumping and trying to grab hold of his ankle.

It was now five minutes until teeth-brushing time. If Elliott was going to goof off with his friends, it was now or never.

18

On Friday morning, as Nory hurried to get dressed, she felt hopeful. She had spent the whole night coming up with a plan, a most extremely awesome plan that would *definitely* get her kicked out Dunwiddle.

It involved the bag of frozen cranberries she had found in the kitchen. *Mwahaha.*

She left a note for Dalia and Hawthorn on the kitchen table and walked to Sage Academy in the early morning light. She slipped through the fence that opened onto Sage property.

Up ahead was the Hall of Magic and Performance, where the dreaded morning assemblies were held. Nory marched to its back door and then carefully,

secretively,

sneakily,

left a trail of cranberries from the back door of the hall to the skunk garden.

Done and done, she thought, sprinkling the last of the cranberries in front of the garden door.

Next step? Get the hidden key.

The step after that would be to free one skunk. One skunk, and only one.

Yes, Nory wanted to get kicked out of Sage and then sent in disgrace back to Dunwiddle.

Yay, disgrace! Yay, Dunwiddle!

But she didn't want to cause real damage to the Hall of Magic and Performance. Nor did she want to humiliate Father so much that he stopped loving her or whatever.

Not that he would. But.

So, one skunk (and one skunk only!) would be

released at exactly 8:58. Two minutes before morning assembly began.

Nory checked her watch. 8:56.

She checked her watch again. 8:57. Okay, then. She took a breath for courage and stepped forward, brass key in hand.

"Ready, skunks?" she said.

"I don't know," said the skunks. "For what?"

Nory whipped around. It wasn't the *skunks* who had answered her. It was—

Oh, for the love of pudding. It was Lacey Clench, arms folded smugly over her chest and eyebrows raised.

"Wha'cha got there?" Lacey asked, jerking her chin at the key.

Nory hid the key behind her back. "Nothing."

"Is this your new plan to get expelled?" Lacey asked. "Since your skunkephant was a dud?"

"Listen, Lacey," Nory said. "I know you hope you'll get my spot once I'm gone, but guess what? That doesn't mean I have to tell you what I'm up to."

"You do know that the only reason you got in is because your dad's the headmaster," Lacey said.

"No. If I was going to get in because of my dad, I would have been accepted the first time I applied."

"Yeah, but—"

"Exactly," Nory said. "But I didn't get in, because my magic wonked out. And then, at Dunwiddle, I got better at fluxing. And this time, when I took the Big Test, I did puffer fish. And mosquito." Nory put her hands on her hips. "So you know what? I think I'm pretty qualified, actually."

Lacey huffed. "The wait list should determine who gets in."

"Maybe yes, maybe no," said Nory. "But guess what? I have no say in that. My dad *is making me* take the spot. And now I have to find a way to get booted, so please go away."

"Are you going to let the skunks free?" Lacey pressed. "Is that it? And they'll all run around and, I don't know, spray your dad with skunk spray?" She barked a mean laugh. "Not a bad plan, actually. If your dad got skunked? In front of everyone? He. Would. *Die*."

Nory grew faint. Lacey was right. Father *would* die of humiliation if the skunk happened to spray him. He'd be even more humiliated than on the great hide-and-seek night, when Sebastian found him cross-legged on top of that filing cabinet!

She gulped. "I'm not going to do it after all. I changed my mind!"

"Oh, Nory," Lacey said. She was already close, and now she came closer. "I think those little skunkies want out pretty badly."

"No, they don't," said Nory. "They like it in the garden."

"But you *want* to get booted," said Lacey. "You said so yourself. I'm *helping* you, Nory." She stuck out her hand. "Hand over that key behind your back."

"No!" Nory stepped away.

Lacey stepped forward. "Go on and give up," she said. "You can't stop me."

Nory popped the key to the skunk garden into her mouth.

"Ew," Lacey said with a grimace. "Germs much?"

Nory ignored her. She'd flux into a bluebird, that's what she'd do. Then she'd add elephant! She'd be a giant elephant-sized bluebird, and she'd flap her wings at Lacey and run her off!

She took a deep breath and fluxed. *Pop pop pop!*

She fluxed, yes, but not into a giant bluebird.

Instead, she was *Tiny*-Bluebird-Nory.

What? No! A *tiny* bluebird was not going to be any use in a battle against Lacey Clench! She was so tiny that the key stuck out of her mouth. It was so heavy she couldn't even fly.

Lacey held out her hand, flicked her fingers, and shot a burst of flame at the key. Ow! The key grew hot in Tiny-Bluebird-Nory's beak.

"Tweet!" Tiny-Bluebird-Nory cried, spitting it out.

"Ha-*ha*!" Lacey cried. "Your magic might be

fading here at Sage, but not mine!" She grabbed the key and waved it triumphantly.

Nory popped back to human form and scrambled to her feet. "Lacey, don't let the skunks out!"

Lacey shoved the key into the lock, twisted it, and *clink*! The bolt sprang open. Lacey opened the door. And not one,

not two,

but *all* the skunks came rushing out, noses twitching and tails swishing.

The skunks ran for the cranberries.

All the skunks.

All the cranberries.

"Noooooooo!" Nory cried.

19

oday's morning assembly was about an Important Historical Flyer who did important historical things. Usually, Elliott enjoyed morning assembly. But today he had a hard time paying attention. He kept thinking about how today was his last day at Sage.

There would be no more assemblies, no more hanging out with GJ and Mitali, no more tips from Dr. Vogel about how to strengthen his flare magic. No more expensive Hex gloves to borrow. No more fun in the dormitory, no more delicious lunches and post-presentation cookies, no after-school band and eight-piano music classes. No more double-talent affinity group, no more beautiful gardens.

At the podium, Dr. Horace's eyes bulged. His neck turned red.

Now his face was turning red! He was saying something, but his words were hard to make out.

"Is this part of the lecture?" Pepper whispered to Elliott.

"I have no idea," he whispered back.

Dr. Horace dropped his notes. His gaze was focused on the back of the auditorium. He looked horrified.

Elliott turned and looked over his shoulder. *Oh, zamboozle!* There were lots and lots of skunks—skunks!—storming the hall.

"Pepper!" he whispered. "Small animal alert! Pause your magic *now*!"

Pepper screwed her eyes shut and pressed her fingers to her temples. "Are those skunks?"

"Yep," said Elliott, standing for a better view. There were two dozen skunks at least, and more coming in behind. And they were . . . dancing?

No, not dancing. But they were chittering and chattering and spinning in circles. Some of them were jumping into the air like circus performers.

They ran onto the pews and then down the lengths of them, hopping from one kid's lap to the next. The students screamed.

Skunks and kids and teachers ran everywhere, like wind-up dolls going ten times their normal speed.

"This is mayhem!" Elliott cried.

"Fuzzies!" yelled an upper-grade Fuzzy teacher with a handlebar mustache. "I call you all to action! Calm the skunks!"

"We're trying!" yelled a girl Elliott recognized. It was Dalia, Nory's sister. "But we can't! They're skunk-drunk!"

"They've eaten *cranberries*?" the teacher said.

"It seems that way, sir!" cried Dalia.

"Oh, no," moaned Pepper, her eyes still closed to pause her magic. "Skunks go wild for cranberries! This is bad, Elliott!"

On the stage, Dr. Horace was doing a funny little jig as half a dozen skunks ran toward him. "I don't like you!" he said. "I don't like you at all, skunks!"

The skunks didn't seem to like the headmaster, either. Those on the stage turned their bodies in unison, all of them pointing their bottoms at him.

In unison, they lifted their tails.

Elliott flung out his hands and wiggled his fingers, channeling all his ice magic on the clouds of gas puffing out from the skunks' rear ends.

Twelve skunk stinks were frozen mid-stink!

Twelve *frozen* skunk stinks clunked onto the stage like hockey pucks.

One spun like a quarter before finally coming to a rest.

"Whoa!" said one kid.

Other kids joined in, marveling at what Elliott had done.

"How did he do that?"

"I never saw ice magic before."

"Is he upside down?"

"He saved Dr. Horace."

"What happened?" asked Pepper. She opened her eyes.

Elliott frowned. Pepper couldn't pinch off her fiercing magic for long, and as she looked at the frozen skunk stinks—she un-pinched it.

Her fierce magic flooded the room. Elliott could tell, because the skunks went even more wild.

"Reeeek!" trilled the skunks. "Reek, reek!"

And now, in a mass, they stormed the stage. All of them!

They scurried up the velvet curtains to a long, high beam above the stage. They clustered there, shrieking and trilling and waving their fluffy tails.

And spraying.

Elliott did his best to freeze the stink juice raining down, but he couldn't get it all. Some stink splashed onto the floor, on the students, and on the velvet seats of the hall. Kids held their noses and stumbled toward the exit.

"Flyers!" cried an upper-level Flyer teacher. "Fly up and capture the skunks at once!"

"No way!" said one Flyer.

"Not a chance," said another.

"Too gross!" cried a third, and that seemed to be the general consensus. Every Flyer Elliott saw continued to push toward the exit.

"You have to help them get down!" Pepper begged, shaking Elliott's arm. "They're scared of heights! Please?"

Then she ran outside with the rest of them, no doubt getting herself and her fierce magic as far away from the skunks as possible.

Elliott made his way toward the stage, weaving in and out of the frantic stream of students. The skunks chittered and trilled. Elliott bit his lip, then flung out both hands and called on his ice magic once again.

Whoosh!

Slurp!

It took a lot of effort but a slide appeared, connecting the high-up beam to the stage below. An ice slide.

The students who were still there oohed and aahed.

"Phew," said Elliott. He hadn't made anything like that before. The fire breathing practice really was making his magic strong. It was a breakthrough.

"Go on!" he called to the skunks. "You're okay now! Slide, skunks, slide!"

The skunks stayed where they were.

They wouldn't go down.

Did they hate ice?

Were they really scared of heights?

Did they think they'd get hurt at the bottom?

What was Elliott supposed to do now?

20

Nory stood at the main door of the hall, staring at the chaos.

It all was her fault. *She* had laid the trail of cranberries. *She* had taken the secret key to the skunk garden.

Yes, Nory had tried to stop Lacey from letting the skunks out, but if Nory hadn't led Lacey to the skunk garden and basically spat the key straight at her, then the skunks would still be safe and sound.

Ooh, ooh, she had an idea for how she could help!

She could flux into some flying animal, then fly up to the skunks and convince them to go down the slide!

Yes! That would work! Wouldn't it?

Dritten! She would do dritten!

She took a deep breath and focused on fluxing. *Pop pop!* She felt fur and paws forming.

Now for a bit of dragon. *Shwoop shwoop!* She had wings! They felt lighter than usual, but they were there, she could feel them!

Okay, then. She launched her body and flapped her wings. Only . . . she didn't fly.

Ugh! Was she tiny again?

No. She could see that her kitten body was its usual size.

Maybe she needed a running start?

Dritten-Nory ran down the center aisle, pumping, pumping, pumping those wings, but she couldn't get off the ground.

Zamboozle, her wings weren't strong enough!

She glanced over her shoulder.

Ohhh. Her kitten body was its usual size, but her wings were tiny. Much smaller than usual.

It seemed that Lacey was right about her magic fading at Sage. Tiny skunk. Tiny bluebird. Now, tiny dragon wings!

The whole Sage environment, with its rules upon rules, its mean table monitors, its uniforms, its superboring assemblies, its scolding teachers and narrow ideas about magic was just TOO MUCH!

Nory felt hopeless. She popped back into her human self and found herself on her butt, in the middle of the aisle. "I hate this place," she wailed. "Everything's all messed up, and I can't get my magic to work, and there's no way to fix *any* of it!"

"Whoa, whoa," Andres said. He stood beside her in the aisle, wearing his brickpack. "You can figure out a solution. You always do. You're Nory Horace!"

Nory sniffled. "Am I, Andres? *Am* I?!"

Andres exhaled. "Okay, here's what we're going to

do. We're going to put whatever this is"—he swirled his hands to indicate the messy and teary hopelessness of her—"on the back burner. Right now, we're going to solve the skunk problem."

He sounded so sure of himself. Nory hadn't felt sure of herself since . . . well, since starting at Sage. She nodded and dragged her hand under her nose.

"Can you still do skunk?" Andres asked.

I doubt it, Nory wanted to say. But no. Being negative would only make things worse.

Self-pity, later. Solution, now!

"I . . . think so?" she said. "It might be tiny, though."

"Tiny will work. If you do skunk and I fly you up," Andres said, "you can show the skunks how to go down the slide. Maybe they'll copy you."

Smart idea. Teamwork! Nory took another deep breath and then fluxed into skunk.

Sure enough, it went tiny. She was the size of a teacup. But she didn't despair.

Andres picked up Tiny-Skunk-Nory and slipped out of his brickpack.

Up, up, up they flew, right to the beam where the skunks were losing their minds.

Andres deposited Tiny-Skunk-Nory near the top of the slide. The real live skunks wouldn't let Andres touch them, but he hovered nearby and made encouraging remarks. "The slide won't be that cold." And, "It's just for a minute." And, "Don't spray me, mister. I'm on your side! I want you to be nice and comfy back in your garden."

Nory inched her way onto the slide. The skunks were still looking wild. They were hopping from foot to foot and their eyes were bugging out. It was only a matter of seconds before one sprayed the entire hall or—horrible, horrible—fell off and plunged to its death. Nory desperately needed them to follow her to safety.

Follow the leader! she tried to say with her paws. *This is how it's done.* She shimmied onto the ice and—oh, wow, was that cold on her bottom—and *whee!*

She slid down, turning midway to see if the skunks were following. And one was! He really was!

It was Domino. And after Domino, came Penguin. Woot! C'mon, everyone, follow Tiny-Skunk-Nory, your teacup-sized leader!

As she reached the bottom, Tiny-Skunk-Nory saw that someone had placed a cozy blanket-lined box at the base of the slide.

Plop! She landed in it comfortably and quickly climbed out.

Domino landed next, right into the box. He yawned and drowsily made his way to the corner and passed out. Penguin did the same. Nory wondered why, and then noticed her sister, Dalia, hovering over the box. She was making the skunks sleepy!

All thirty skunks slid down the slide, one by one.

All thirty skunks landed in the box and promptly fell asleep.

Nory fluxed back into a girl. The disaster was over.

"Gracious," Father said, flickering into view next

to Nory. "That was something. Where is that boy . . . Cohen! Mr. Cohen, where are you?"

Elliott cleared his throat from a few feet away. "Um, here?"

"Yes. You. The icing of the odors was quite impressive. Showed real initiative. And that slide! Well done with the slide."

Elliott turned pink. "Thank you," he mumbled.

"And Nory."

"Yes, Father?" she asked.

"Thank you for going up there. None of the other Fluxers thought to do it."

"I couldn't have if Andres hadn't helped," Nory said. "I tried to do dritten and fly up myself, but . . ." Her words trickled off as her hopeless feelings trickled back in.

"What I want to know, however, is how the skunks got out of the skunk garden in the first place," Father said. "And cranberries? Who on earth was so foolish as to give them cranberries?"

Nory's heart dropped from her chest to her stomach, and then from her stomach to her toes. She had never, ever meant for this to get so out of hand.

There was an upside, though. Once she confessed to Father, she would be expelled for sure.

"I was the foolish one," she said bravely. "It was me."

21

Father sent the rest of the teachers and students off to shower and change. Then he led Nory to his office and closed the door.

He sat behind his desk and buttoned his suit jacket. It made him look as official and angry as he could possibly look while smelling of skunk spray.

"Well?" he said.

"I'm sorry, Father," Nory said, her cheeks burning. "It was my fault the skunks got out and ate cranberries."

"What?"

"I was planning to let just one out! Not all thirty! And actually, I changed my mind at the last minute, but—"

Nory broke off. She hated Lacey. She really did. But she had a feeling that Lacey was mean and bitter mainly because of being so unhappy. Unhappiness changed people. And strange though it seemed to Nory, she knew that what Lacey wanted most was to go to Sage Academy.

Why should Nory ruin that for her, when maybe a happy Lacey would be a nicer Lacey?

Plus—double rainbows with sprinkles on top— if Lacey went to Sage, *then Lacey wouldn't be at Dunwiddle any longer*!

She told Father about the morning's string of disasters as best she could, leaving only a few small details out.

"So anyway, yeah," she finished. "I ended up in way over my head."

"Indeed," said Father, his voice icier than the slide. "Do you know how irresponsible your behavior was?"

"Yes, Father," Nory said.

"Do you know how embarrassing, how personally humiliating, your behavior was? To me?"

"Yes, Father."

"Then why?" he demanded. "Why would you do such a thing?"

"Well . . ."

"Did you think it would be amusing?"

"No, I—"

"How could you possibly think skunk odors would be amusing?"

"I did it so you would expel me!" Nory blurted.

Father appeared to be speechless, but only for a moment. Then he threw his arms in the air. "Why would you want to get expelled from Sage?"

"Because!" cried Nory. "I want to go back to Dunwiddle! I asked you—nicely!—if I could please go back, only you ignored me. Didn't you see how weak my magic was, from trying to fit into a 'box of normal' instead of learning to work my unusual talents? Don't you see that I feel like crying all the time?" She tried to steady her breathing. "I'm not happy here. I had to make you see that, and the skunks seemed like the best way!"

Father rubbed his eyes with the backs of his hands. "Don't be dramatic, Nory. No one's 'happy' every minute of every day. You'll toughen up. It might take a few months, but you will."

Nory's chest tightened. "Wait. Does that mean you're not going to expel me?"

"Well . . ." Father hesitated. "Technically, you're not a student here yet. I don't have to expel you. You can go back to Dunwiddle until after the winter break and then you'll start at Sage for real in January."

Nory swayed. She steadied herself by grabbing Father's desk.

Father didn't notice. "I trust that you have learned your lesson—and that you will never do anything like that again."

There was a knock at the door.

"Come in," Father said.

This was it? The meeting was over?

No way! Nory couldn't stay at Sage. She wouldn't!

"No, no, no," Nory begged. Spots swam before her eyes. "Please send me back. Please! I don't like it here! It squashes me and forces me to be something I'm not. I'm losing my Nory-ness!"

"I think you should listen to Nory, Father," Hawthorn said, stepping into the room. He put his hand on Nory's shoulder.

"Me too," said Dalia. Her fingers found Nory's and squeezed. "I mean, I miss her," Dalia explained. "But this place isn't right for her. Did you see her dritten? It couldn't even fly!"

Nory nodded, weak with relief. *Dalia* saw her.

"Her magic is getting worse here, not better," Hawthorn said. He regarded Nory with concern, and Nory smiled. Hawthorn saw her, too. "At Dunwiddle, it was different. That Upside-Down Magic class was helping her, Father."

Father looked back and forth between the three of them.

"You know I shouldn't be here," Nory said,

borrowing a bit of courage from her brother and sister. "I need to be in Dunwiddle."

Father held out for several tense seconds. Then he threw up his hands again and said, "Fine. *Fine.*"

Nory's heart drummed against her ribs. "Fine, what?"

"You can return to Dunwiddle," he said. "This is clearly *not* the right place for you." The way he said it stung, but Nory would take it.

She was going home.

"I have some work to do," Father said abruptly. "But you three should use the gym showers. Do you have extra clothes in your lockers?"

Hawthorn and Dalia nodded.

Nory didn't have a locker. Oh, well.

In the hallway, Nory threw her arms around her brother and sister. "I'll never forget what you did in there."

Even though they all stunk like skunks, they hugged for a very long time.

22

It was Friday afternoon. Classes were over and Elliott was packing his stuff before the bus left at six. He had already returned the Hex glove to Dr. Vogel. He left his borrowed uniforms in the dorm room laundry hamper. There was a knock on his door.

"Come in!" he hollered.

"Mr. Cohen? May I speak to you for a moment?"

It was Nory's dad! At Elliott's door! What was he doing there?

"Um, sure?" Elliott put down the pajamas he was folding and opened the door. The headmaster seemed very large inside the small dormitory room.

"Take a walk with me," Dr. Horace suggested. "I was hoping we could have a chat."

"Sure," squeaked Elliott. "Let me just find my shoes."

"I'll wait for you outside."

The two of them wrapped scarves around their necks and strolled through the campus as a light snow twinkled down, making everything seem new and fresh.

"Mr. Cohen," Dr. Horace said, "I heard you've been attending the double magic affinity group."

"I only went once, sir," said Elliott. "I was invited by a fellow student." He didn't want to say Mitali's name in case she wasn't supposed to have invited him. "I know I'm not really a double talent. I think they were just, you know, being welcoming. The students here have excellent manners."

Dr. Horace was silent. They passed the snow-dusted topiary garden.

"Dr. Vogel reports that you've made huge progress in Flare class this week," the headmaster finally said.

What? Elliott had thought they were talking about how he'd gone to a meeting he shouldn't have gone to. What did this have to do with Dr. Vogel?

"She said that with a little extra support, use of Hex gloves, and possibly a tutor to help with your unusual style of magic, you could be very successful here at Sage," Dr. Horace went on.

"Did you say *here at Sage?*"

"I'm not sure if you have heard yet, but a spot has recently opened up in the fifth grade."

"The spot Nory's taking."

"The spot Nory will *not* be taking, actually."

Elliott blinked. When did this happen? Did Nory know?

"She and I decided that she should go back to Dunwiddle," Dr. Horace said.

"Wow." Elliott was happy for Nory. He knew how

badly she wanted to return to Ms. Starr's friendly classroom.

"So, Mr. Cohen," said the headmaster, "we are wondering if you would like the spot."

Elliott stopped walking. "Me?"

"Yes. You."

"But . . . what about Lacey? She says the spot should be hers. Isn't she next on the wait list?"

Dr. Horace looked confused. "Lacey Clench? No. We don't even keep a wait list."

"But Lacey said . . . she said her dad told her she was first on the wait list. She said so lots and lots of times."

Dr. Horace fluttered his fingers. "Humph. Perhaps her father wanted to soften the blow of not getting in. But, no. Miss Clench is not Sage material."

"And I am?"

Dr. Horace nodded. "You would officially join us after winter break. You should speak to your family and make a decision together. We are prepared to offer you a full merit scholarship, including free tuition, room, and board. We had some big donors this year and one of our goals is to attract more double talents to Sage Academy." He put his hand on Elliott's shoulder. "We would be honored to offer you the top-level education your talent requires."

Wow. Wow. Wow.

Elliott was relieved that Dr. Horace didn't expect an answer right away, because he had no idea what to say.

Nory rode back to Dunwiddle with the other UDM kids on Dunwiddle's dilapidated old bus. The ride was bumpy. The heat hardly worked. The plastic covering on Nory's seat was ripped, revealing the yellowing foam beneath. When Nory dug her fingers into it, she pulled out a crusty, dusty choco fire truck that must have been decades old.

She was too happy to feel grossed out. She was too happy to do anything except bounce a bit on her seat and soak in the passing scenery.

Farewell, Sage! she thought.

She would miss Hawthorn and Dalia. And her Fluxer friends.

And she'd miss Father. A little. Every so often.

But she would not miss Sage. Not one bit.

The bus went around a curve, and all at once the rolling hills smoothed out and the town of Dunwiddle came into view. Nory's breath caught. Her heart swelled. She grabbed Pepper's hand and squeezed. "Pepper, look!"

Pepper leaned toward Nory's window. "Oh, yay," she said softly. "Hi, Dunwiddle."

Soon Nory would see Aunt Margo! And Figs, Aunt Margo's boyfriend. And Nory would see her bedroom, her beloved little green bedroom in her beloved aunt's beloved house. And Monday, she would see Ms. Starr and Principal Gonzalez, and Coach, and all her kittenball friends! The flood damage had been repaired, according to Nurse Riley. The school was back to its crumbling, disheveled self.

"Nory?" Pepper said. She tugged to free her hand from Nory's grasp.

Nory held tight. "Yes?"

"Ew. What's in your hand?"

"What's in *my* hand?" said Nory. "*Your* hand!" Silly Pepper.

"Yes, but what else?" Pepper tugged harder, and Nory let go.

Oh. The choco fire truck had melted between their palms, squeezing out of its red foil wrapper.

Pepper wrinkled her nose. "Gee. Thanks."

"You're welcome," Nory said cheerfully. "It's only seventy years old. You should totally eat it."

"Pass," Pepper said.

Nory turned back to the window, tingling all over with happiness.

She was almost home.

The next Monday, Elliott woke up early because his brother, Ezra, toddled into his room, climbed on his bed, and squeezed Elliott's nose.

Ahh, home.

At Sage Academy, no one had squeezed his nose. Everyone woke up to the ting-a-ling of a bell rung by a dorm supervisor, followed by a gentle knock on the door. Then there was the bustle of kids, pushing to get a spot at the sink and rushing to the cafeteria for breakfast.

But home was still nice. When Elliott and Ezra went downstairs, their dad had folk music playing in the kitchen. Their mom was wearing her white doctor's coat and drinking coffee. "Dr. Horace wants our answer this morning," she reminded Elliott, handing him a plate with sliced apple and peanut butter toast.

Elliott nodded.

He ate breakfast. He went back upstairs and got dressed for the day. He played blocks with Ezra. Then his dad took Ezra out in the stroller so Elliott and his mom could have a quiet house for the video call with Dr. Horace.

It hadn't been easy making this decision. There were so many things to think about.

Elliott's palms were sweaty. His heart was racing. Was he making the right choice?

Brrring!

Dr. Horace answered from his office, wearing a suit and tie. "Good morning, Mr. Cohen. Dr. Cohen."

Elliott's mom said good morning. Elliott did, too, but it came out as a croak.

"So," said the headmaster. "I trust you're ready to give me your decision?"

"We are," said Elliott's mom.

"I'd like to hear from Mr. Cohen himself," said Dr. Horace. "Elliott, will you be joining us here at Sage?"

Elliott breathed deeply to steel his nerves. He opened his mouth to answer.

Join Nory, Sebastian, and friends in their
next adventure:

UPSIDE*DOWN MAGIC #8: NIGHT OWL!

Acknowledgments

It probably goes without saying that the skunks in this book are heavily fictionalized. Cranberries don't make them silly, and they're probably not scared of heights. You don't want to try to pet them unless you're a magician.

Many thanks and a bigged-up chocolate pudding to the team at Scholastic, including but not limited to: David Levithan, Rachel Feld, Maya Marlette, Taylan Salvati, Lauren Donovan, Lisa Bourne, Sue Flynn, Melissa Schirmer, Robin Hoffman, Lizette

Serrano, Emily Heddleson, Abby Dening, and Aimee Friedman.

Gratitude and a plate of Rose Parlor cookies to Laura Dail, Barry Goldblatt, Tricia Ready, Elizabeth Kaplan, Eddie Gamarra, Lauren Walters, and Deb Shapiro.

Hot chocolate with alphabet marshmallows and much appreciation for all the pixie dust and mouse magic to our team at the Disney Channel: Lauren Kisilevsky, Charles Pugliese, Nick Pustay, Josh Cagan, Suzanne Farwell, Susan Cartsonis, Joe Nussbaum, and the wonderful cast, crew, and designers.

A bowl of delicious cranberries to Bob, who couldn't be more awesome.

We are grateful to our families: Randy, Al, Jamie, Maya, Mirabelle, Alisha, Daniel, Ivy, Hazel, Todd, Chloe, and Anabelle. We wish we could take you all with us to the skunk garden!

Finally, much love to our readers. We hope you like this glimpse into life at Sage Academy, and that you let your magic shine, whatever kind it is.

About the Authors

SARAH MLYNOWSKI is the author of many books for tweens, teens, and adults, including the *New York Times* bestselling Whatever After series, the Magic in Manhattan series, and *Gimme a Call*. She is also the co-creator of the traveling middle-grade book festival OMG Bookfest. She would like to be a Flicker so she could make the mess in her room invisible. Find her everywhere @sarahmlynowski.

LAUREN MYRACLE is the *New York Times* best-selling author of many books for young readers, including the Winnie Years series, the Flower Power series, and the Life of Ty series. *The Backward Season* is the most recent book in her Wishing Day trilogy. Her co-authored book, *Let It Snow*, is a movie on Netflix. She would like to be a Fuzzy so she could talk to unicorns and feed them berries. You can find Lauren online at laurenmyracle.com.

EMILY JENKINS is the author of many chapter books, including *Harry Versus the First One Hundred Days of School*; *Brave Red, Smart Frog*; the Toys Trilogy (which begins with *Toys Go Out*) and the Invisible Inkling series. Her picture books include *All-of-a-Kind Family Hanukkah*, *A Greyhound, A Groundhog*, *Lemonade in Winter*, and *Toys Meet Snow*. She would like to be a Flare and work as a pastry chef. Visit Emily at emilyjenkins.com.